# BILL'S MAGIC BOX
## II

October 2024
First Hardcover Edition

All rights reserved.
No part of this book may be reproduced
or used in any manner
without the prior written permission of the copyright owner.
Copyright © R.C. Hammond
Bill's Magic Box LLC, PO Box 6782
Denver, CO 80206

Publisher's Cataloging-in-Publication data

Hammond, R.C..
Bill's magic box II / R.C. Hammond.
Denver, CO: Bill's Magic Box LLC, 2024.
Twenty rhyming short stories for children.
LCCN: 2024915463 | ISBN: 979-8-9901730-1-9
LCSH Short stories. | Children's poetry, American.
BISAC JUVENILE FICTION / Stories in Verse
LCC PZ7.1 .H36 Bil 2024 | DDC [Fic]--dc23

# BILL'S MAGIC BOX
# II

R.C. Hammond

# Once Upon A Babysitter

Some babysitters are good.

Some babysitters are bad.

Some babysitters don't care.

Some babysitters get mad.

Some babysitters will let you eat dessert,

some of them will not.

I'm sure that most of my babysitters

never liked the job they got.

The turnover rate for babysitters

is rather very high,

which means at the end of the night

it's the final goodbye.

Having a sitter never come back

has become a normal thing.

They're never fully aware

of the terror I bring.

They come into my house with a smile on their face

that by the end of the night I've all but erased.

Like the sitter I had the other night,

I don't think she'll be back, and I bet you I'm right.

It was the two of us

watching the television

when she said, 'I'm having a friend over

and I'm going to watch TV with him.'

Well I never heard her ask my parents

if she could have a friend over with her,

and I wondered if she had asked them

they would have let that occur.

I asked her, 'Did you tell my parents?'

'No,' she said, 'but they probably wouldn't care.

Besides, babysitting is easier when it's done in pairs.'

She was probably right about that

but immediately a plan I did hatch.

I said to the TV from my perch on the couch,

'I don't think my parents would want

a stranger in the house.'

'He's my friend,' she said.

'Still,' I said.

And before she could talk any further

I said, 'If you let me have a friend over

I'm sure it wouldn't be a bother.

Isn't it fair that if you have a friend over I should have one too?'

I kept on talking while she was thinking it through.

'My parents always let me have sleepovers

(which was sort of the truth),

and I'm sure they wouldn't mind

if I had one with you.'

That last part might have been a little lie.

But soon I had two friends over

with me to spend the night.

'I thought you were only going to have *one* friend over?' she said.

'No,' I said, shaking my head.

'Two little people equals one big person, right?'

She rolled her eyes and blew out her cheeks.

'I guess,' she said with a sigh.

'The best television,' I pointed out, showing her through a door,

'is this one right here. This one on the second floor.'

I told her this though I knew quite well

that the best television was in the basement

where my friends and I would dwell.

I set her up with the movie channel

so she and her friend would stay put,

so down in the basement and on the first floor

she'd never have to set foot.

Which would be stupendously awesome

for my friends and me

because we'd have two floors and the kitchen

to rule over for the night, you see.

Not only that, my friend Ted has a phone

his parents let him use in case he needs to call home.

Which happened to add another layer

to our already awesome situation

and keep the babysitter from having to move

from her babysitting station.

'If you're worried about us,' I told her,

'and you just want to check in,

you can get on your phone

and give Ted's phone a ring.

So you and your friend can watch your entire show

without needing to get up and visit us below.'

She looked confused when I said it and asked,

'Is that normal for your sitters?

To call you on the phone while they sit upstairs?'

'Of course!' I blurted. 'It happens all the time!'

Making sure my smile shined.

'It makes babysitting super easy

and why all my babysitters really like me!'

'Hmm,' she said, with a look that showed

she had some particular doubt.

'You see,' I said, shutting the door,

'from this room you'll never have to come out!'

I could tell she was skeptical by the look she was giving,

and that my plan, perhaps, she wasn't fully feeling.

'Yep!' I shouted, from behind the door. 'You can just let us be!

We even know how to make our own mac and cheese!'

Which we did! And it was fun!

We didn't even do the dishes when we were done!

She phoned us a few times when she heard the pans rattle.

'What's going on down there?' she asked.

'It sounds like you're having a battle.'

'Nope! All's well! Dinner was great!

By the way, how's your date?'

'It's not a date,' she said, 'he's just a friend.'

I found the smiley emoji on Ted's phone

and with my thumb I pressed *send*.

I guess their movie was good because we got no more calls,

and during those hours our play got more involved.

It started out with having a place to hide

in case the babysitter ever tried

to leave the upstairs and find us.

Then whatever the issue, we wouldn't be there to discuss it.

Away from the wall we moved the couch,

made a roof with a blanket

and under it we crouched.

It slowly grew into something grand

with rooms and halls

we crawled through on our knees and hands.

But that was quite a bit ago.

Since then our hiding place has grown

from a great big fort to a giant a castle.

It's amazing what one can accomplish

without babysitter hassle.

In fact I would say our play reached new heights

when the three of us all became knights

with our own kingdom and gold to protect.

We even had a government elect.

The room on the first floor has a bed with a giant mattress

that became the drawbridge for our gold-protecting fortress.

It took some time to shove it down the stairs,

and we only made a couple of tears,

but in the end the mattress door stood up tall

and took up the entire basement hall.

It made a perfect drawbridge to drop over our moat

and later became the deck to our boat.

We also found a closet that was equipped

with blankets and sheets for our ocean-bound ship.

To protect our gold we had to set sail

if we knights and our kingdom would ever prevail.

That's when we became pirates of the sea

and set out to steal everything we'd need.

Like the clothes it would take to look like pirates

that we found rummaging through my parents' closet.

With Dad's ties wrapped around our heads,

and the boots we found under the bed,

and Mom's skirts around our waists,

and her makeup covering our faces

we were the scariest pirates the world has ever seen!

Then we pillaged the kitchen and took all the ice cream.

During the night it just so happened

Ted's phone we left behind.

We thought we heard its ringing chime

but Ted's phone we could never find.

Which was okay because knights and pirates had no such things

in the olden times.

After ice cream we played videos after moving the TV

far back into the President's room where the television should be.

We turned up the sound as loud as we could

so the explosions would shake our fort as explosions should.

If we had been quieter I'm sure we would have heard

the babysitter claiming in so many words,

'Oh my Gosh! What a mess!

Your parents aren't going to like this!

The house looks like it was hit by a tornado!

Where did those kids go?'

She came down to the basement

yelling for us to clean up,

but behind our mattress door

we just piled up more stuff.

Quietly we found hiding places in the hull of our ship

and put hushing fingers to our smiling lips

motioning to each other to be real quiet

until the babysitter got sick and tired

of yelling for us.

Until she gave up.

Until we could hear her feet

walking above our heads,

having given up in defeat.

Ted's phone we found

on the bathroom ground

so the rest of the night

we gathered tight

to watch videos on the phone.

We even heard the shuffling above

when my parents came home.

We stayed super quiet

and pretended we were asleep,

and stayed like this until above us

we didn't hear a peep.

We watched more videos

and laughed about a bunch of stuff.

(I had to quiet my friends

when the noise became too much.)

We stayed up way past our bedtime.

(When Ted's phone died it was past midnight.)

We woke up not knowing where we were,

the night before being kind of a blur.

Mom served us pancakes

without being mad,

although she did comment on the night we had had.

'How was the babysitter?' she asked us all.

Dayton said, 'Great!' with his mouth full.

'Yes! Great!' Ted and I agreed.

'It appears to me that she let you guys do whatever you pleased.

And I wonder who talked her into having a sleepover?'

she asked, giving me the once-over.

We all shrugged and went back to our eating,

and after my friends left

the day was kind of deceiving.

I thought my parents wouldn't be too happy

with how things went the night before,

but they never said a thing

as they cleaned and picked things up off the floor.

But now I stand here, and now I get it,

as I watch my parents put on their jackets.

Standing before me is my next sitter

looking crusty, sour, and bitter.

I've met her before

back when I was four.

She's a friend, they say, of my grandmother's,

but I'd call her a witch if I had my druthers.

'Bye!' my parents said, in voices oh so cheery.

'Make sure he gets to bed on time,'

they said to Mrs. McLeary.

'Oh, he will,' the old woman said, giving me a glare

that sent a shiver down my spine from her evil stare.

After a long meal of silent tension

(she made me sit with her without watching the television)

she sent me to bed.

And the sun hadn't even set.

So I'm lying here feeling some unrest

(my stomach rumbling from her goulash

I'm trying to digest)

staring at the ceiling wondering what I'm going to do

about my babysitting life

being permanently in doom.

I'm thinking about and pining for

all those babysitters from my past,

wondering how on earth

I'll ever get them back.

# Surviving The Lava

I think I remember my dad coming in

to tell me I had to get up.

The weekend was over,

Monday was here,

which makes getting up kind of rough.

I can jump out of bed at the shake of a stick

if I'm headed to a plate of pancakes thick,

or cartoons on Saturday,

or football on Sunday,

then I wouldn't feel so sick.

But Monday and school?

Getting up for those two?

It makes me want to stay in bed

and never have to move.

But my father shouting,

'You better be up! We're leaving soon!

If you don't eat now

you won't eat until noon!'

had me opening my eyes

but just barely.

(Why does school have to start so darn early?)

Yawning and stretching I sat up in bed

when a burning smell

suddenly hit my head.

I heard bubbling and gurgling

and the heat was horrendous,

when I looked below me

what I saw was stupendous!

My floor was covered in lava!

How deep I didn't know!

Again my dad shouted,

'Hurry up if you want to eat before we go!'

I yelled back a feeble, 'Oka-a-ay!'

at my bedroom door,

wondering how I'd get dressed that day

without ever touching the floor.

I had to think about every move,

every turn and twist,

for if any part of me touched the ground

that part would be burned to a crisp.

I jumped off my bed, and onto my chair,

counted to three, and sprang into the air.

To get to the window was my goal,

and I wouldn't have made it, truth be told,

but I caught myself, and stopped my fall,

with a foot on my skateboard leaning against the wall.

(That went up in flames as it left my foot

leaving a cloud of crackling soot!)

I felt the heat from the hot lava's glow

from the embers snapping and popping below

as I shimmied across the windowsill

and jumped on top of my dresser.

Pulling my clothes out from above

was nothing less than a disaster.

I watched a sock fall and flare into flames,

and a pair of underwear do the same.

With my clothes in a wad, and only one hand to hold,

I had to ease my way off of the dresser

and be brave and bold.

To get to my door

over the bubbling floor

that was spitting balls of fire,

I had to skim the edge of the floorboard

as if walking a high wire.

Through the hallway the lava flowed

and covered the entire floor.

I made it to the bathroom

by hanging from the doors.

I knew I wasn't safe

when the lava my foot nearly chafed

after I slipped from the tub

while giving my teeth a scrub.

The lava flowed down the stairs

like a slow-motion waterfall

and spilled through all the balusters

as fire lapped the walls.

I inched across the rail, and slid down the bar,

making the stairs for me

the easiest to maneuver by far.

(I'm a master slider.

I've been sliding down the banister since I can remember.)

But then came the hard part:

how I'd make it to the kitchen.

I jumped on a chair

to observe the situation.

The lava was now hotter than ever,

and to not touch the floor I'd have to be clever.

A spectacular move I'd have to deliver

to get to the kitchen over the hallway lava river.

I had to get up my nerve, and focus my aim,

to reach the top of the closet,

and hang from its wooden frame.

I launched from the chair as far as I could

like a movie stuntman from Hollywood.

One hand caught the frame

but my other hand slipped.

Just then I was thinking, *Oh, no! This is it!*

*I'm going to land in the lava and be burned alive!*

*No! It can't happen! I'm too young to die!*

With all of my might

I pulled up as hard as I could

and was able to grab the frame's

thin edge of wood.

I was breathing hard,

hanging by my fingertips,

wondering how long I could hold on,

hoping my hands wouldn't slip,

when I looked between my arms

to see what my next move should be,

and there were my dad and my sister

staring up at me.

(It was kind of weird,

but for whatever reason the lava disappeared.)

My little sister was giggling, but my father wasn't.

'Jimmy, what are you doing?' he grunted.

'We're leaving. Now.

Once again you missed breakfast

…somehow.'

They both passed around me and went out the front door

so I figured it best if I dropped to the floor.

In rapid haste

with a smile on my face

I grabbed my stuff and caught up to them,

happy I survived

the lava again.

# Where The Stars Fall From The Sky

There's a place where the stars fall from the sky,

where a little girl does lie.

They don't land with a boom,

they don't land with a crash,

they land with a quiet *poof*

in the soft warm grass.

By herself,

all alone,

she's the only one who knows

how to get there on her own.

It took her many tries to find

the place where there is only night.

She didn't find it right away,

many times she went astray.

She hit dead ends

time and time again;

on many paths

she'd have to turn back.

Until at last

she found a path

that only she can follow.

She crawls on her knees through a tree that's hollow,

tiptoes through a grotto where shadows wallow,

balances on a log that teeters and totters,

skips over rocks surrounded by water,

climbs up the crag of a sheer cliff side,

and shimmies along its edge with careful foot slides,

swings from a tree using only a vine

to a grassy hillside she must climb.

In the last glow of daylight,

on top of the hillside,

down she'll lie,

and close her eyes.

She'll give herself a little push.

She'll hear the grass pass with a whoosh.

Faster she'll roll, faster and faster,

feeling the ground and the grass rush past her.

Faster she'll spin, and faster she'll roll,

over the ground getting steeper below.

Faster she'll roll, and faster she'll spin

until the ground starts to give in.

And just when she feels nothing below her,

and nothing to hold her,

and that she'll never recover,

and fall forever…

the land will bend,

and she'll feel earth once again.

She'll slowly roll to a stop,

in the thick warm grass her body will flop.

She'll lie very still, and feel the world spin,

until her head and body are one again.

She'll open her eyes

to a night sky

full of so many stars that twinkle and glitter

they reflect on her face like water's shimmer.

In the soft grass, under this nighttime sky,

in the complete silence of the warm summer's night,

she'll hear a swooshing through the air,

and feel a soft breeze through her hair.

Her eyes will alight

from the star falling bright.

This is the place where the stars fall from the sky

where only she does lie.

They don't land with a boom,

they don't land with a crash,

they land with a quiet *poof*

in the soft warm grass.

Soaring down in golden arcs

they land around her in splashing sparks.

When a bountiful bunch has fallen her way,

and her body is nearly covered,

she'll burst forth and start to play

in the land only she discovered.

She'll laugh, and sing, and jump, and slide

over the hills of shimmering light.

She'll gather stars

into her arms

and throw them above her

creating a glimmering, sparkling cover.

She'll take one at a time

and toss it into the night,

and watch it fall back

with a splash.

As the stars fall on

they'll make a pond

deep enough to swim in.

She'll dive in,

and through the stars she'll swim,

like a mermaid through the heavens.

After a heart-full time well spent,

she'll find a special star, and begin her voyage again.

She'll take the star with cupped hands from the pocket of her dress

and put it in her jewelry box on top of an old clothes chest.

She'll open the drawer

and look inside,

and different colors the star will shine.

When it starts to lose its glow,

she'll take it out, soft and slow,

and out her window

let it go.

Like a bird - she'll watch it fly -

back into the starry sky.

She'll follow her path, and return again,

her adventure she'll retrace,

to the land where darkness reigns,

and the world touches outer space.

She's the only one who knows

how to get there on her own,

the place where only she will lie

where the stars fall from the sky.

They don't land with a boom,

they don't land with a crash,

they land with a quiet *poof*

in the soft warm grass.

# The Crow Knows

This might sound confusing

but your brain you will be using

to work the situation out.

For if you can get to the end

that is when

you'll be putting a treat in your mouth.

(But the treat isn't easy to get to.

You'll have to think it through.)

Imagine the finest cupcake,

the tastiest one to your liking.

Vanilla, or chocolate,

or raspberry cream

covered with custard icing.

Maybe it has candy sprinkles,

or it's topped with butterscotch,

or has a whipped cream center

with a cherry on its top.

Imagine this cupcake

sits high on a shelf,

too high for you to reach by yourself.

But there's a small step stool in the closet

that'll work for the task so you take it out and use it.

You step up once, you step up twice,

until you're at the very top.

You reach as high as you can

but before the cupcake

your hand must stop.

The step stool isn't tall enough,

it just won't work,

but you remember there's a ladder in the basement

hanging on a hook.

The basement's locked and it needs a key,

and you think about where that key might be.

You remember the key hangs on the side of the closet

and with the step stool

you can reach up and grab it.

You use the step stool to get the key

to unlock the basement and set the ladder free.

But there's another locked door, and then another,

and you need different keys to open the others.

So you use your step stool three different times,

and in the last room the ladder you find.

You take it upstairs with the best of care.

(Leaving some nicks where the walls were bare.)

And that ladder, oh yes, it's tall enough!

You grab your cupcake and your mouth you stuff!

You're smiling and happy knowing you weren't beaten

from getting to the most delicious cupcake you've ever eaten!

Now think of what you had to do,

how you had to think it through;

all the decisions you had to make

to get to that tasty cupcake.

You even had to use some tools:

the keys, the ladder, and the step stool.

Well, it so happened, a few of the human race

once put a crow on a similar chase.

They placed some meat in the back of a box

that was guarded by bars as kind of a lock.

The crow couldn't reach the meat with its beak,

it needed a tool to get to the meat.

So they hung a stick on the end of a rope

that the crow could use to prod and poke.

The crow took the stick to poke through the bars

but the stick in its beak didn't go that far.

The stick for the crow was just too small,

with the stick in its beak it couldn't reach the meat at all.

But those humans, those scientists, those crafty folk

hid another stick for the crow to poke.

They put a longer stick inside a see-through box

that could only be released by dropping in rocks

down a tube one at a time,

like a gum ball that's released with a drop of a dime.

It would take the weight of the three rocks

to open the door on the box

that held the long stick

that the crow could pick

to use as the tool to hold in its beak

to pull out the meat.

But the rocks were also placed behind bars

that the crow could reach, they weren't too far,

if it used the first stick held in its beak.

Each rock the crow would be able to reach.

After prodding out each rock

the crow put the rocks

down the tube on the box.

The door opened, the long stick was released,

and the crow used that stick to get its treat with ease!

Eight different moves the crow had to do

and in the end the crow did prove

that it was more intelligent than we humans thought.

Perhaps it's a lesson we should all be taught.

For what's in a brain we know not.

But it's a brain all animals got.

So if a crow knows how to use a tool

maybe it knows other things too.

And the crow isn't the only animal that knows how to use tools,

chimpanzees and parrots know how to use them too.

Remember that using a tool means thinking it through.

Would a crab or an alligator know what to do?

A crow can even recognize a human face.

This was determined after a few scientists were squawked at and

chased.

Scientists who were studying them, and perhaps bothering a few.

The crows even recognized the same scientists

after a year or two.

So next time you come upon a murder of crows

(that's what more than two are called if you didn't know)

maybe they'll recognize you and know just who you are,

and you should get to know them and learn their call.

Because we really don't know what the crow knows…

But perhaps if you become its friend

you will be the first to know.

# What's In A Name?

If you know the crow then you know how crows go.

In a *murder* is what we've been told.

But how about others that take to the sky

in large groups when they fly by?

Like bats, or buzzards, or geese?

Or owls, or parrots, or bees?

Did you know a group of bats is called a *colony, cloud, cauldron,* or

*camp*?

And buzzards fly in *wakes*? (Do you like the sound of that?)

There's a *gaggle* of geese. A *parliament* of owls.

A *pandemonium* of parrots. (Is it because they're so loud?)

Have you ever seen a *swarm* of bees,

thousands clumped upon each other hanging from a tree?

(I think I'd rather get my honey from the store

than have a bunch of those guys stinging me.)

Crocodiles like to *bask* in the sun,

that's what they're called when there are more than one.

Sharks swim in *shivers*, cobras slither in *quivers*.

(Just the thought that makes me quiver and shiver.)

Imagine a rhinoceros crashing through your room.

If it were a *crash* of rhinoceroses you might meet your doom.

What if you had a *colony* of rats under your floor?

Or a *nest* of snakes in your bottom drawer?

Or a *shrewdness* of apes knocking at your door?

If you had a *stench* of skunks

all of those things

might not bother you anymore.

In the desert you might find camels in their *caravan*,

or a *colony* of ants in the sand.

In the jungle you might find an *army* of frogs

croaking together upon a log.

Or a *shadow* of jaguars hiding in the shadows.

Or *bales* of turtles in watering holes.

Or a bloated hippo thundering by.

A *bloat* or a *thunder* are hippopotami.

Have you ever seen a flamboyant flamingo standing on one leg?

A *flamboyance* or a *stand* is the name they all take.

A *prickle* of porcupines is understandable.

A *troop* of monkeys might be uncontrollable

unless you put them in a barrel.

A *barrel* of monkeys might be more bearable.

It would be fun to see elephants in a *parade*

with a *drove* of donkeys keeping the pace,

and a *leap* of leopards leaping behind

with a *band* of gorillas keeping the time.

Some of these names they kind of make sense,

like a *tower* of giraffes looking over a fence.

I can see a *cackle* of hyenas cackling around their prey.

If I saw a *pride* of lions I'd get out of their way.

It's possible a jellyfish could smack you on the face.

But if you swam into a *smack* of jellyfish

you might want to swim the other way.

But not into a *fever* of stingrays,

that might ruin your day.

Unless a *turmoil* of porpoises shooed them way.

I wouldn't want to be ambushed by an *ambush* of tigers

or a *pack* of wolves.

And fish might not be the smartest

but they're trying their hardest

which is why they always travel in *schools*.

Perhaps a *business* of ferrets are always busy,

and a *conspiracy* of lemurs are always planning a conspiracy.

A *labor* of moles might get the job done.

A *romp* of otters would be kind of fun.

But other names seem sort of odd.

Would you call a group of whales a *gam* or a *pod*?

And a *clowder* of cats?

What's that?

A *sounder* of swine, and a *drift* of pigs?

Who made up those names and what were they thinking?

Did someone see a *knot* of toads tied up in knots?

Or kangaroos robbing a bank and that's why they're called a *mob*?

With a *gang* of turkeys and weasels involved?

A *sleuth* of bears might get the crime solved.

There's a *cete* of badgers, and an *obstinacy* of buffalo,

and I'm asking myself, 'Where did my dictionary go?'

But what's in a name? I guess we should have fun

naming things when there are more than one.

So if there were more than one of you out there

what would you name them?

Would you travel in a scurry, or a horde, or a bevy,

or some other thing?

I think if there were a bunch of me's we'd all be called a *couch,*

because all of this naming

has worn me out.

# The Legend Of Windmill Willy

Legend has it he was born into life

floating like a balloon

somewhere in a mine

far below a saloon.

Instead of having to hold him up

his mother had to keep him down.

It was the strangest birth they ever had

in that now non-existent town.

It was in the 1800's when things started to fall apart,

and from that town in the middle of nowhere

people began to depart.

By the middle of the century all that existed

was a population of thirteen.

In the church book it was listed.

The town was built on barren land,

not a tree in sight,

only rocks and desert scrub

in a searing white sand's light.

Building the town was quite a feat,

hauling wood across the desert's heat,

but eventually a town was formed

with all the necessities that would give it charm.

A baker, a dentist, a man who cut hair,

a cobbler, a farrier, a woman who built chairs.

There was a bank, a post office, and a general store.

One really needed no more.

For the town had a mine, and the mine had gold,

and the gold could buy everything that was sold.

The townspeople were wealthy,

poverty didn't exist,

and for a very long time

it lasted like this.

Through the years the town grew in size

and became a spectacle to the eyes

with theaters, and saloons, and festivals galore.

The town became one of fabulous lore.

But all the prosperity that made it thrive

had but one thing that kept it alive.

And then one day word came from below

that down in the mine

there was no more gold.

Could it be true,

could such a thing occur?

Well they dug, and they dug,

but there was no more gold for sure.

And it was on that same day

when the bad news came

that the weather in town

began to change.

It was a breeze that blew,

oh so slight,

that drifted into town

in the dead of night.

And it didn't slow,

it kept on growing,

without the people even knowing.

The breeze blew into the next day,

the next, and the next,

and it slowly picked up speed

as it blew into the next.

There seemed to be a relationship

between the wind and that desert town,

for the more the wind picked up

the more the town broke down.

People began to leave,

jobs they came to a halt,

because there was no more gold

with which the people could shop.

It was a rapid decline,

people left in droves,

except for a woman and her man

watching her tummy grow.

They had to stay, they couldn't leave

until their baby came.

For they had the baby that floated about.

Willy was his name.

By the time that Willy was born

the town had become a ghost

with empty troughs, and horseless hitching posts,

tipped over wheelbarrows,

and curtains fluttering from open windows.

A brass snap clanked on a flagless pole,

fireplaces sat empty and cold,

dusty floor boards twisted warped and black,

rusty pots hung above mouse-eaten grain sacks.

Doors hung crooked on their hinges,

and the desert sand piled up by the inches.

The people that stayed were too weak or too old,

for them it would be too dangerous to go.

And the wind that never stopped

became so very fierce

its nighttime growling and hurricane howling

was piercing to the ears.

The sand that blasted hurt the skin

and that's why everyone lived within

the crags of the earth and the caves of their mines.

In the dark underground

they spent all of their time.

With no electricity and lights at night

they lived by the flicker of candlelight

hoping that one day the wind would end

and they could live on top of their land again.

The only reason they still survived

was because of a windmill that kept them alive.

A windmill that pumped water from on top of a hill

and sent it down to the people for their cups to fill.

And while the days passed and the wind blew stronger,

Willy was growing longer and longer.

But he never got heavier,

he never gained any weight.

In fact he got lighter

day after day.

And his parents couldn't have him floating about,

they were too worried he'd get blown out

and be whisked away from the mine forever.

That's why they kept him on the end of a tether.

Everything was fine until the treacherous day

when all of the water went away.

For the desert had become a dangerous place,

and the furious winds had all but erased

everything that stood above ground.

Including the windmill that spun around.

It was the windmill that provided them water.

Without the windmill their days were over.

And leaving the mine was not an option -

it would only cause certain destruction.

Thirst began to take its course,

and those that were left were thinking the worst.

To live without water just can't be done.

People got sick, one by one.

Willy, who watched it all from above,

couldn't stand to see those that he loved

getting sicker and sicker by the day.

But there was nothing he could do

or he'd be blown away.

The relentless wind that kept on growing

was now underground with its blowing.

People started to fear for their lives

as the wind blew through the caves day and night.

There was no escape from the impending disaster

as the ferocious wind blew harder and faster.

And then one morning people awoke from their sleep

to find Willy's tether piled up in a heap.

All were crying as they gathered around

Willy's rope upon on the ground.

They all knew Willy had been blown away,

sucked by the wind right out of their cave.

Everyone claimed that this was the end

for without water and child they couldn't pretend

that they could survive in their caves any longer

as the penetrating wind blew stronger and stronger.

With itchy eyes, and blistered lips,

coughing and groaning in dry-mouth fits,

they were all about to call it quits

when from their spigot they heard a drip.

They gathered around the communal basin

with looks of surprise on their faces.

Their water once again flowed!

How it was happening they didn't know!

But they quenched their thirst until they were stronger,

and all of them were sick no longer.

Now if one listened closely to the howling outside

they would hear another cry.

They would hear Willy whooping it up

because he was no longer in his cave tied up.

It was as if Willy was born for the wind

for it had a different effect on him.

After Willy was blown out of the cave

(some would later claim

that he planned it that way)

and blown through the air day after day

across the desert far away,

he discovered quickly how his body was made.

He learned to use his body as a natural sail

which was why he was so happy, and laughed, and regaled.

He could fly through the treacherous winds

like a fish through water if you could see him!

He rigged himself up

to the shattered windmill pump

that the wind had all but broken up.

How much he loved to spin around

and know he was providing water from the underground.

Back in the cave his mother could swear

that she heard him outside but she couldn't bear

the thought of her son and what happened to him

as she wept to herself in silence within.

Then one day during a terrible gust

in blew Willy in a cloud of dust!

To whistling cheers, and happy tears,

Willy told them all to have no fear.

As he floated above his parents and friends

he told them their troubles were about to end.

Outside a covered wagon he had built

with what was left of the town and the old windmill.

Now the ending has it to this tale

that Willy harnessed himself up as the wagon's sail

and sailed his people from the desert's harm

to be cradled once again in civilization's arms.

And legend has it that to this day

if into that barren desert you stray

and come upon the place where the town once was

the air will start to flutter and buzz.

A breeze will start to blow back and forth

until it reaches a magnificent force.

And if closely to the wind you listen,

to the whishing, the whooshing, the howling, the hissing,

a faint sound you will hear,

a whooping, or a hooting, or a crying cheer.

As the wind blows harder

the laughter will get louder

until it surrounds you

and echoes all around you.

You'll feel like you're in a grand cathedral hall,

a cathedral with the largest organ of all

that blows a hymn through underground walls

where Willy hails and laughs along

with the old gold mine and its ancient song.

That's when you'll know you're in that special place

where something existed that had been erased,

where a glorious thriving town had been.

Where Windmill Willy still plays in the wind.

# The Pond

There's a place not far from my home

where no one really likes to roam.

A place enclosed by a rusty fence

where the land is so very dense

with plants, and bushes, and lots of trees

that sometimes I have to crawl on my knees

and move branches away from my face,

and sometimes my path I'll have to retrace.

Some days I'll wonder if it disappeared forever

as I search through the bushes packed together.

But then the ground will start to get boggy,

my shoes will start to get soggy,

and through the leaves I'll suddenly see

a shimmering from the pond,

and I'll wonder why it was so hard to find

and why it took so long.

For the pond's not small,

it takes up a lot of ground.

It's about the size of a basketball court

and almost perfectly round.

Maybe that's why no one's ever here

because it's hidden away.

Or maybe the pond only comes out when I look for it.

(That's what I like to think, anyway.)

Little islands of deep thick grass that I must carefully land upon,

for if I don't and I step in the mud, my entire foot will be gone.

And those little round mounds

that make gurgling sounds

I can't stand on for too long or they'll sink into the ground.

But I stand on one just long enough to find my favorite spot -

an open area next to a rock.

The only place I can walk along

where the ground is hard next to the pond,

where bushes and branches aren't a bother.

I can also stand on the rock and look into the water.

It's surrounded by cattails

and I like to pull one out when I get there.

I take out the fluff and whip it to an fro,

believing with my magic wand

I can make it snow.

With the cattail stick

I make it kick

mud up under the water,

as I scrape it around

it trails a muddy cloud

like I'm a speeding desert marauder.

I stand up tall to look for a fish to spear.

(I saw a big one the last time I was here!)

But I don't see one

so I take my javelin

and throw it like an olympic decathlete,

but it's hollow and light

and spins off in flight,

and ends up landing behind me.

(Making the strider bugs scatter in fear.

How they're able to walk on water

to me that's not very clear.)

Slithering over the mud, a salamander leaves a trail

of its stomach, toes, and tail.

A dragonfly balances on a blade of long grass,

its wings look like clear stained glass.

A butterfly passes and there's a cloud bugs

so small they look like dust in the sun.

I dip my hands in the water

to catch a tadpole or two,

but when I sit up,

lifting up my hands that are cupped,

all they do is fall through.

The minnows I try to catch

by making a cave with my fist.

They look inside

but away they glide,

never fully falling for it.

That's when I see two eyes

that before were disguised

and I see the shape in the sand.

I grab a handful of mud,

and other crud,

and now there's a toad in my hand.

I rinse him off and get him clean,

I look at him and he looks at me.

I wonder what he's thinking

while his eyes are lazily blinking.

I put him in the pocket of my shirt

where he won't get hurt

while around the pond I roam

before I take him back to my home.

I jump off the rock and move along

continuing my walk around the pond

because I always find something new.

Like the time I found

a nest on the ground

and eggs that were black and blue.

I thought I saw a beaver once,

a muskrat, or a mole,

whatever it was it was brown and furry

when it ducked into its hole.

And speaking of ducks

it's just my luck

to see an entire family.

A mother, a father, and little green chicks

floating together happily.

I look for food to feed the chicks

and from a raspberry bush I pick

a handful of berries and get as close as I can.

(The rest of the day I'll have red ink hands.)

I toss the raspberries toward the chicks

but the chicks just paddle away.

Watching the raspberries land with a splash

they must think I'm throwing rocks their way.

And I don't want them to think that

so I just eat the rest that I have.

While I eat

something moves by my feet

sliding through the grass.

I see the path it takes

because the grass blades shake

as the unknown thing goes past.

I follow the shaking blades

and the scraping sound they make

until the grass blades no longer shake.

Have you ever held a snake?

I didn't think I had what it takes

but the garter isn't poisonous

so I know my life's not at stake.

I reach down quickly and grab its tail

and hold it in the air,

and watch it glide back and forth

with its unemotional stare.

With my other hand I hold it lightly

so it can still move so not very tightly.

I feel its skin that's silky and cool

and all its muscles when it moves.

I watch how fast its forked tongue flickers

and softly stroke its body with a gentle finger.

That's when the toad jumps out of my pocket

and the snake shoots at me like a rocket!

It happens so fast

I stumble back

and sink in deep

as the cold water creeps

through my pants

and my jacket sleeves!

My feet are stuck

in the heavy muck

because there's no foothold or handhold

in the mud that's thick and cold,

and there's nothing to push off of

and nothing to hold onto!

I feel like I'm stuck in glue!

The earth makes slurping sounds

like it wants to suck me down

and keep me there forever!

*I'm slowly going to sink*

*and never be discovered!*

I dive for a clump of grass

and pull as hard as I can.

The grass is strong

so I can pull myself along,

and though I get free

there's still mud up to my knees.

I hold on to the bushes and sapling trees

until I feel hard ground at my feet.

My heart's still racing

thinking about the snake chasing

the toad in rapid haste

and how fast

it snapped

when the toad jumped from my shirt to my face.

As I stomp off the mud on solid ground

I remember the sound

of the hissing snake snapping at my head.

Instead of the toad

it could of been my nose

the snake could have eaten instead.

But the toad got away,

and the snake went its way,

and I decided after this day

I'd take a holiday

from having animal stowaways

and let the animals stray

in their own way

before it's me that becomes the prey.

(If you've ever had a snake

snap at your face

a similar decision you might make!)

With small bubbles squishing out of my soles

my walk back home is soggy and cold.

In my house I can't hide

although I try

but the squeaking screen door turns Mom's eye.

Even from the kitchen

she can see my condition.

That's when I know

I'm in for a scold.

But I don't tell her what I had to go through

and what I had to do

just to recover a shoe,

and why I'm dirty and cold

from a mud bog that nearly swallowed me whole,

and that a snake nearly took off my head,

and I'm lucky to be alive and not dead.

No, I don't tell her these things

because I'm thinking something else instead.

While she's telling me irately

that my behavior is less than stately,

and mad because I'm muddy and wet,

wondering why I don't understand the rule yet

about being home from dusk to dawn,

asking why I was gone so long,

and something about my school clothes being on,

I'm thinking that after school tomorrow…

I'm going back to the pond.

# Snow Day

I'm lucky my city has seasons

and here's one of the reasons.

In the winter my town can get real cold,

and sometimes it will start to snow.

Sometimes it will snow a lot,

so much so everything comes to a halt.

On those special days a meeting will be held

by the school superintendents and those who ring the bell.

For if it's too dangerous for the school bus,

and perhaps too difficult for the rest of us

to get to school safely without incident,

in the morning a message will be sent

that school will be closed for the day.

That's when I jump up and yell,

'Snow day! It's a snow day!'

I slam down my breakfast at a furious pace

while Dad inquires over his newspaper with a curious face,

'I wonder why school can't be met with such glee?

That child's mood has changed one hundred and eighty degrees.'

It will take too long to get out the door

as I try to find my snow clothes from the year before.

My boots won't fit, my snow pants will be too tight,

my hat will itch, it just won't feel right.

But all that disappears when I go out into the snow

and jump off of my steps wondering how deep it goes.

I land with a *Whumpf!* and a grin on my face -

the snow is at least up to my waist!

In the street

the snow is so deep

no cars can even drive by,

and the cars that are marooned

look like sand dunes

with their snow piled so high.

It's peaceful and calm with a soothing silence,

only the snow falling off of the trees breaks the quiet.

I watch the snow flow around my waist

as I pick up my pace

and run as fast as I can but it's not very fast

because of all the snow, my boots, and my big thick pants.

I run and I launch as far as I can

(although it's not very high I still leave land)

and dive in head first.

But it doesn't hurt

because the snow is soft and fluffy.

It buries me completely

turning everything I see white!

That's when I realize there are places where my clothes aren't tight.

When I stand up to shake it all off

buried in the snow I see some cloth.

One of my mittens

that's gone missing.

With snow down my pants, and now down my back,

from all of the snow that just fell off my hat

I retrieve my mitten and dump out the snow.

And even though my hand is really cold

and the inside of my mitten's wet,

there's no way

I'm going inside yet.

My thoughts are on the garden wall

that I climb up until I'm ten feet tall

and jump into the snow

yelling, 'Geronimo!'

*Fumpf!* - covered in snow again.

But I get up and do it again and again

until there's only one soft spot left

that hasn't been trampled down yet.

Off I jump

but I don't get up.

I look at my heavy breathing

going into the air

like a smokestack flare

all the white smoke that I'm heaving.

I try my best to blow smoke rings

but it's harder than I think,

so I make my breath go as far as I can

like a fire-breathing dragon.

A big handful of snow I put in my mouth

but only a little bit of water comes out.

I eat more snow because I'm kind of thirsty

while I watch the snow fall all around me.

When I look into the sky

thick white flakes fly past my eyes

making me feel like I can fly.

But it's hard to keep them open wide

and not to squint

because when the flakes hit

it stings a bit.

I try to melt the flakes

with my breath before they hit my face.

But I can't

and feel my pants

getting wet from sitting in the same place.

Because I've been sitting in the same position

I'm melting the snow and water is entering.

My snow pants aren't exactly waterproof.

They used to be a few years ago, I guess,

but now they've lost their *oomph*.

It's a wet snow,

not a dry snow,

the kind perfect for making snowballs.

Sometimes when it's really cold outside,

and the snow is dry,

I can't make snowballs at all,

even if I pack it hard

the snow just falls apart.

But this snow is perfect for packing

and snowman stacking.

But I don't make a big snowman,

I make a lot of little guys,

and stand them on the wall, side by side.

Behind a tree

I pile snowballs next to me,

and in one big flurry

launch them in a hurry,

like a rapid-fire cannon

until no snowman standing!

In the corner of my yard

there's still snow that's not packed down hard.

Deep fluffy powder

I decide to push together

and make an igloo

with a round door that I can crawl through.

After a couple times of caving in

I'm soon digging so far within

that my whole body can fit inside.

I turn to see only my boots sticking outside.

But the walls are turning into ice

from my warm breath I'm blowing inside,

and to make the room bigger

I have to take off a mitten and scrape with my fingers.

(With the other hand that's not so cold and wet.

At least not as cold as the other one yet.)

There's not a lot of space

for my arm to move and scrape

while resting on one shoulder,

and it's kind of dumb

because now those fingers are numb

and both of my hands are now colder.

So I put on my mitten

and take to hitting

until my hand goes completely through.

Without making the wall crack

around the hole I pack

until I have a window with an outside view.

It just so happens my window looks out upon

the kitchen in my house,

and I see Mom carrying something hot,

something with steam coming out.

My head drops onto my arms

because there seems to be less charm

in being in here than being in there

where it's nice and warm.

One of the longest walks you can ever do

is to trudge back home when snow day is through.

When everything is wet,

and everything is cold,

and your entire body is frozen solid.

And I'm close to tears trying to take off my boots

because my hands are so cold they can't even move.

Mom says something about staying out there all day.

(It's true, I didn't realize the sky was turning gray.)

As she's pulling off my wet clothes inside out,

and I'm so cold and tired I'm about to pout,

she says something that makes my eyes go wide

about a grilled cheese sandwich with tomato soup on the side

she says I can have if I go put on warm clothes.

Where I find the energy to run to my room and to the table so fast…

who knows.

But as far as a perfect snow day

that's how one goes.

# Prune

It happened in the middle of summer

during the hottest part of June,

Mother said that if I stayed in the pool all day

I'd turn into a prune.

It's a typical thing my mother would say

that doesn't make a lot of sense.

Sure my skin gets wrinkled a bit

and looks like it's full of dents,

but turning into a *prune*?

Isn't that a fruit?

How can a kid do that?

It just didn't compute.

Really, she has to know what it's like

living in a desert town

in the middle of a bunch of scrubby hills

with nothing else around.

Who in their right mind

would pick a desert to live in,

besides my very own mom,

and who knows what she was thinking.

So it's really not my fault

that I'm stuck in a sweltering town

where my favorite part of the day

is when the sun goes down.

I don't know about your backyard

but my yard shakes and bakes.

It's nothing but gravel and cacti,

and rocks hiding poisonous snakes.

So what does Mom want me to do?

Go out into the desert and play?

And turn into a pile of white skeleton bones

like those animals that lost their way?

But there she stood above me

with her hands on her hips.

'Maybe you should get out of the water,'

she said, 'and take a break for a bit.'

I have to say

our community pool

is the greatest thing ever invented.

During a hot, searing summer day

it's where I want to spend it.

Even though it's full of kids

splashing this way and that,

and it's hard to find a peaceful place

to float upon my back,

and sometimes I get kicked,

and water splashed in my eyes,

there's always a place underwater

where I can hold my breath and hide.

I like to feel the nice cool water

smothering me like a blanket.

(I think if I were a dolphin

I'd probably really like it.)

Mom was saying other things

because I could see that her mouth was moving,

and by the angry way she was looking at me

there was something she was disapproving.

But within all the ruckus and splashing about,

'I can't hear you!' was all I could shout.

She said something again,

shook her head,

and waved her hand in defeat,

so I dove under water,

did a handstand on the bottom

so all she could see was my feet.

Back again, I was,

in my wonderful underwater world,

watching my hands make bubbles

the faster I spun and twirled.

I dove around, and swam about,

and blew water out of my mouth,

pretending I was a whale

exhaling a pluming spout.

I was a shark, and an octopus,

and an underwater sea diver.

(Even though it stung my eyes

I kept them open underwater.)

I knew that this day of swimming

was going to turn out to be grand

because I had only one goal in mind

and that was to never touch land.

So that's what I did.

I never came out.

Even during Adult Swim

I secretly swam about.

I'm not sure how time is made

or why it goes so fast,

and why my swimming days

never seem to last.

I never realized the sun was setting

and I was the only one in the pool.

I never realized I had shrunk in size

and had to be fished out with a netting tool.

But that's what happened

and before I knew it

I was placed in a mason jar,

and put on the counter

for all to observe

on my kitchen bar.

'That's Henry,'

my mom now says, pointing to my jar on the counter.

'He never wanted to leave the pool,'

and closer to me her friends wander.

They stare at me through the wavy glass

with looks of fear and sadness,

wondering how on God's green earth

such a thing could pass.

They mumble and they murmur

in their confused states of dismay.

'All he wanted to do,' Mom explains,

'was stay in the pool all day.

I told him and I warned him

that if he didn't leave the water soon,

his body would shrink and shrivel in size

and he'd turn into a prune.

But did he listen to me?

He certainly did not.

Does he ever listen to me?

He certainly does not.

But maybe if he did listen to me

he wouldn't have gotten what he got.'

So now I'm borrowed by all the moms

with their vigilant frowns

and placed on checkered picnic blankets

on our swimming pool grounds.

I've saved all the moms the bother

for when it's time to come out of the water

they just hold my jar up high.

They don't even have to try.

When their children see my state

they leave the water without complaint.

(I think most of the moms in town

believe I'm some kind of a saint.)

I'm sure I should have listened better

and done what my mother had said,

and not stayed in the pool all day,

and left the water instead.

Because now I'm paying the penalty

for that dreadfully hot day in June,

when I didn't listen to my mother,

and I turned into a prune.

# The Dodo

The Dodo bird is no longer with us,

and as of late, it hasn't been much discussed.

As of, perhaps, three hundred and sixty years

because that's how long the bird has been 'disappeared'.

The last time anyone saw a Dodo was around 1662

on an island in the Indian Ocean, give or take a year or two.

Yes, the Dodo bird was once a living thing

but now it no longer exists,

which means that at one time it once was

but now it's called 'extinct'.

It might have been one of the very first times

in the minds of humankind

to realize that if there's a lack of respect,

and if mankind is going to neglect

a certain animal's habitat,

that animal might disappear forever,

and never come back.

For instance, the Dodo,

one of our first examples,

a bird that at the time we found it

seemed a little pampered.

Closely related to the pigeon

but what a big pigeon it was.

Maybe because its life was so chill

was why it became so large.

Three feet tall on average, and about thirty pounds,

and even though it had wings on its body

it couldn't leave the ground.

A tranquil island it found

with nothing else around

until some humans anchored a boat

on the island's sandy ground.

The boatmen were hungry and needed to eat

because they ran out of food while crossing the sea.

They found a plump bird that couldn't fly,

so they thought they might give that bird a try.

And as time went on more people arrived

looking for something to keep them alive.

But it's been said that the Dodo wasn't very good eating…

So was the Dodo bird's extinction because of human feeding?

Or was it because of other guests

that the Dodo might have considered a pest,

traveling with their human companions

and making a home when upon landing?

Pigs, or dogs, or cats, or rats,

or the macaque monkey who likes to eat crabs?

Island visitors that competed for food,

and maybe ate a Dodo bird egg or two?

Was it one of these or a combination of all

that caused the Dodo bird's fall?

Or was it how the Dodo bird came to be

so fat, so plump, flightless, and carefree?

For it must have landed on the island after flying through the air.

(Scientists doubt they just floated there.)

And if that's the case it means that the Dodo once flew

until it found a cozy island abundant in tasty food.

And didn't need to move,

or fly back over the sea.

What if you found a nice island with yummy food,

would you want to leave?

An island with soft sand beaches

where no bad storm ever reaches

surrounded by waters of crystal blue

with a perfect lagoon for a dip or two;

where there's always a hammock within reach

in case you want to have a little snooze by the beach.

An island with a fine buffet

where you can stuff your face all day, every day

with bonbons, and pancakes, and homemade pies,

hamburgers, and cupcakes, and onion ring fries,

various tubs of puddings and jellos

served with bottomless soft drinks with little paper umbrellas.

Lounging by the pool thinking about your next meal…

Perhaps after a few years *lazy* would be what you'd feel.

So the flying Dodos who took to the sea to roam

found a quaint little island they could call home

with fallen fruits, and nuts, and delicious seeds,

and no other animal with which they'd have to compete;

nothing out there that would eat them, and nothing life-threatening

around…

A place so peaceful and safe

they could even put their nest on the ground.

Is this how they came not to exist?

Living a lazy life they couldn't resist?

Or was it something else on the list?

Perhaps…

Quite possibly…

It could be claimed…

The Dodo bird's extinction was because of its name!

If you were named Dodo

how far would you go?

What about Charlemagne?

Now *that's* a name.

Abraham Lincoln, Julius Caesar,

Joan of Arc, Nebuchadnezzar,

Kamehameha, and Anne Boleyn,

Nefertiti, and Martin Luther King.

(Even Louis XIV has a certain ring.)

There's Catherine, and Constantine, and Alexander the Great.

But so far no one named Dodo

has led the human race.

There's the Siberian wolf and the crocodile of the Nile.

(That reptile has been here awhile.)

There's the lion of the Congo and the Sumatran python.

All these animals are not yet gone.

So maybe if you want your family line

to travel farther into time

don't name your child Dodo.

That would be a no-no.

But let it be said, just to be fair,

that if the human hadn't showed up

the Dodo might still be there.

Even though that's something we'll never know

it does seem like wherever we go

we bring our problems, our issues, and our diseases

while nature's abundance around us decreases.

It's as if in our quest to see everything

we forget about the destruction we bring.

Maybe it's best just to leave some things alone

so animals like the Dodo can have a permanent home.

So animals like the Dodo can call a place their own.

So animals like the Dodo would still be here to roam.

# Lemonade Stand

I sure did it this time

I decked my lemonade stand out to the nines.

Year after year I'm not sure how I get it done

but whenever I have a lemonade stand

mine is number one.

I don't think anyone even comes close

to me as a lemonade stand host.

And I don't like to boast

but everyone should be raising their lemonades to me

as a toast.

Before I dress up and open my doors

there's a lot of work to do before.

As you know if you're familiar with lemonade stands

it takes some time to put one together by hand.

Especially mine with its teak wood counter

that doubles as a bar if customers want to hang out and chatter.

Which is fine with me because that's the point -

the more people gather, the more people stop

and check out my joint.

Customers can schmooze at my bar with its tung oil finish

and polyurethane coat that makes it scratch resistant.

It's rimmed

with gold trim

and has pyrographic inlay designs

of sailboats and seagulls to soothe the mind.

Of course the idea is to get out of the sun

and my yellow canvas adjustable shade system on electronic pulleys

gets the job done.

Sturdy Moso bamboo posts make certain the stand doesn't move, even when my customers are leaning on it, and pushing upon it,

to get closer to my brew.

The base has a tropical lauan veneer

giving the sense that an ocean is near.

(I want my clientele to momentarily forget

that they're sipping their lemonades in the deep Midwest.)

The stiles on the base are a copper plate,

the brass foot rail creates a relaxing state.

There are matching retro double hooks to hang your hat on.

If it gets too hot my automatic misters kick on.

In the background,

through speakers that are mounted,

play instrumental Beach Boys songs.

And let us not forget about the overall presentation.

It's important to have lavish bar decorations.

Like the recirculating fountain

bubbling water down a snow-capped mountain

that looks like Mount Fuji,

while a 75-inch HD

flat screen TV

plays surfing movies.

On the patio is the ice sculpture I chiseled by hand

of two dolphins being ridden by a standing man.

That man being Neptune

holding his trident harpoon.

(If you look closely it's really me,

my icy hair blowing in the salty breeze.)

The fathers that are frequent customers

have their own hanging mugs,

making them feel like they're part of a club.

The children prefer their lemonades served in coconuts.

For the mothers I have crystal fluted cups.

As to say, I have something for the entire family,

but if you come solo you're always in good company.

And though my upper-scale atmosphere suits high-class tastes,

it's the customer service that defines the place.

To have the best lemonade stand in all the land

you have to take matters into your own hands.

Starting with my attire.

I like to look real nice

while I'm delicately handling

a silver tong of ice.

I don the shirt

I wear to church -

a steam-ironed button-down

bleached with medium starch.

With a yellow bow tie

I found online

my look just shouts, *It's lemonade time!*

My seersucker shorts that keep me cool during the day

are probably the reason why most customers stay.

Holding them up and matching my tie

are yellow box cloth suspenders clasped with a brassy shine.

To top it all off I have a boater straw hat.

You can't get more lemonade than that!

Right before I click on

my *Open* sign of yellow neon

I make sure the bar is stocked

with the appropriate *accoutrements*.

Like the platinum bucket ice holder

with elk head handles that are golden

full of ice from my mold trays

(of course free of BPA).

My ice cubes are shaped like roses and diamonds;

I even have ice

shaped like the dice

from Dungeons and Dragons.

But crushed ice

is always nice

and you can get that from my pristine,

and always shiny clean,

stainless steel slushy machine

that crushes the ice

just right.

And some might call me an overachiever

because my ice is made from spring water from Artesia.

I have a potted plant of peppermint,

and one of spearmint,

and cut fresh sprigs for each cup's adornment.

Little paper umbrellas? Sure, I have those.

But my lemonades also come with a boat.

Miniature schooners I made out of toothpicks

with tiny sails cut from lotus flower silks.

When all is ready, and all is prepared,

I click on my sign, and shout, *'Lemonade!'* into the air.

*'Get your lemonade! Lemonade here!'*

'You know you don't have to shout when I'm standing so near.'

Now, I must admit, and be the first to confess,

some of my clients aren't the best.

Like Suzy Marinowsky who lives across the street.

She's always at my stand first it seems

to tell me things that I don't want to hear,

like, 'Can you stop screaming *lemonade* in my ear?'

(To tell you the truth I was pretending she wasn't there

which was why I kept shouting *lemonade* into the air.)

'You can stop your yelling,' she tells me, 'I'm right here.

And why do you keep doing this year after year?

Having a stand that serves lemonade?

You don't even know how lemonade's made.'

That's when I'm inclined to mention

I take lemonade-making to another dimension.

My lemons, I tell her, are Brazilian imports

closely inspected from port to port.

Hand cut, and hand squeezed, it's all hand made

with organic sugar pressed straight from the cane.

'No it isn't,' she says. 'You use a mix.

You can't fool me with your stupid tricks.

The empty box is right there at your feet.'

(I forgot to throw the box away so no one could see it.)

'And I'm not even getting close to your counter

because last year that old board gave me a splinter.

Can't you use something that's not warped and rotten?

You can't even set a cup down without spilling upon it.

Not that you have cups that stand up.

You use those stupid cone-shaped cups.

The same stupid cups they give you at the hospital

whenever there's a pill to swallow.

The cheapest paper cups you could ever have

that if you hold on

for too long

get soggy in your hand.

Which is probably why you never add ice,

because your cups are so small, if you did,

you'd have a drink you could only sip twice.

And you can stand there all day and shout and holler

but there's no way your lemonade is worth a dollar.

And that table for your customers? You might want to add chairs.

What are we supposed to do with that table you have?

Look at it and stare?

Not that's even big enough to sit around

because it's your sister's table she sets her dolls around.

And have you ever thought about taking the time

to make a better sign?

You use the same sign year after year,

it's dirty, and stained, and the corners dog-eared.

It used to be white, I think, but now it's an off shade of yellow,

and not the pretty lemonade yellow, the gross kind of yellow.

And it looks like it was written by someone younger than your age.

The word *Lemonade* starts off big, then gets smaller,

and curves down the page.

The last two letters you can barely see.

And how many times has that sign been blown down the street?'

That's when I'm compelled to say,

'Suzy, are you going to be here all day?

Because I think you're scaring my customers away.'

But Suzy's not done, she has more to say.

'And look at your shirt, it's quite disgusting.

You might want to wear clean clothes before you start serving.

It looks like that T-shirt you just pulled off your floor.

It still has spaghetti sauce on it from the night before.'

That's when I grab a cup

and quickly begin to pour.

'Here, Suzy, take it, it's free.'

Suzy looks at my lemonade, and then looks at me.

She takes it with a twinkle in her eye I can see.

'Thank you,' she nods, and skips away.

Not the best start to my lemonade day.

But I regain my focus and let out a sigh.

*'Lemonade!'* I shout into the sky.

# The Education Of My Avatar

I found an empty school room

just perfect for the learning,

for the lack of intelligence of my avatar

was very disconcerting.

I had recently purchased him

from an online auction,

and he was the best of the bunch

to serve my gaming functions.

He stands twelve feet tall

and about eight wide,

and there's not an ounce of fat

on his furry hide.

Part animal, part robot,

and built like the Hulk,

my hope was that he had some brains

with his muscle-bound bulk.

But it was apparent when I got him

that he was a little slow,

and many things about the cyber world he just didn't know.

And I really need my avatar to be quite versed

and excel at all I need to do

in the metaverse.

For my avatar is really me

so he has to be big, and strong, and smart.

That's why I had him in the classroom -

to work on that last part.

He sat hunched over his classroom table

and didn't fit in his chair,

but classrooms aren't for comfort,

they're for learning, as everyone's aware.

'Okay, avatar,' I said. 'Pay attention, because you're representing me

wherever you go in the computer world

from digital sea to digital shining sea.'

That's when I realized I had my work cut out -

he just sat there staring

with an open mouth.

'I know you're good at slaying dragons,

and you know how to hunt and kill,

but we really have to do some work

on your communication skills.

On certain gaming platforms

you have others on your team,

it's not just you destroying all the monsters,

as fun as that may seem.

You may have to lead a Starfighter fleet,

or grow a field of pixel wheat,

or memorize the rare traits of a horse,

or what a car can do on a certain course,

or run a node,

or create some code.

Oracles, bridging, and how to breed an Axie!

Bartering for Dark Energy on the Opensea!

It would be good to know how to run a casino

with Flux, and Sand, and Mana, and Flow

while battling a Rypper in the Illuvial Sea,

and tokenizing bees for an apiary!

Mazes, and minting, and mining Trillium—!'

That's when I stopped

because I noticed

his lights were going dim.

It wasn't hard to see from the front of the class

that my avatar's eyes were glazed like glass.

His look suggested he wasn't soaking it all in.

He was a bit bewildered, and he had a silly grin,

and there was nothing funny about what I just told him.

But I thought it best not to scold him.

I figured his education was going to take some time.

'I didn't think it was going to be *this* bad,'

I mumbled to myself with a whine.

'Okay, that's enough for the day!'

I told my avatar, 'You can go away!

But be back tomorrow bright and early!

We have a lot of work to do with your learning!'

I planned on a week's worth of class,

and the week went by fast,

and if I had to give him a grade

I don't think he would have passed.

But it was good enough

for most of the stuff

I needed him to do,

while I kicked back

in my hammock

as my stacks of money grew.

You see, the point of having an avatar,

and the reason why I bought him,

was so he could go explore

the many metaverse worlds

and start bringing the serious cash in.

If you're not familiar with p2e

let me further explain.

It stands for 'play to earn'

which means there's real money to be made.

Online games these days

in tokens they pay

that you can exchange for other things

their value brings.

You can trade a plot

on a metaverse lot

next to a beach and a sea

for trending clothes

or I suppose

an nft of a jpeg monkey.

You can go on Solana

and buy a Sollama.

Hop over to Polygon

and trade it for a WavyLong.

Ethereum or Arbitrum

your day is never done

as you shard

or level cards

for a Bandit or Mercenary,

or capture some Ghost on Aavegotchi.

And, yes, all these things

make my head ring

but with my avatar I'll just sing

along with my cash register going *Ka-ching!*

I'll just be counting dollars

which was why I hollered,

'Go get 'em my avatar friend!

Go make me proud

in the computer cloud!

Go be a successful degen!'

(Between you and me

I didn't tell him fully

that the reason I bought him,

and the reason I taught him,

was that he was going to be working for me,

winning games, and juggling tokens,

while I relaxed under a tree.

It's not something I think

an avatar needs to know,

which was why I never mentioned it

and kept it on the down-low.)

And guess what? Avatars can work 24/7!

That's right! This summer! Is going to be heaven!

So I digitized him, and I wished him farewell,

and sent him deep into the cyber world realm.

(Wondering if I should be worried about

that silly grin that never left his mouth.)

Then it happened,

after a week or so,

I checked in just so I would know

exactly how much he was bringing in.

That's when I broke out in *my* silly grin.

I had tokens in my digital wallet I didn't even know existed!

I guess during his schooling days my avatar really listened!

So I mixed myself an ice-filled Kool-Aid

and hit my hammock in the shade

thinking to myself how I had it made

doing absolutely nothing and still getting paid.

And I drifted off

in thought

as in my head I played

various scenarios of me skipping the entire fourth grade.

That's how I spent my wonderful summer

as the days blended into one another.

Until one day I thought I'd check back in

just to count my stacks again.

That's when I felt like I got hit by a train!

And a wrecking ball!

Looking in my online wallet

there was nothing in it

at all!

'*What?* This can't be!'

I shouted frantically

as I pounded my computer keys.

I couldn't find him! My avatar just disappeared!

I looked through all the games,

on all the exchanges,

went on every platform,

and scrolled through hundreds of pages.

Was he off on a mission? Has he been deleted?

Removed from cyberspace because he cheated?

I searched and searched for days and days,

through sleepless nights, my mind in a craze.

My computer screen started to look like haze

when one night I clicked on an advertisement page

that led to a full-screen image of his face.

I nearly fell out of my chair!

There it was! That vacant stare!

Clicking on I went weak in the knees -

my avatar had done something I couldn't believe!

He had created his own metaverse!

Just like Mark Zuckerberg!

And in order to enter

I had to pay!

That's when I claimed,

'Insane!

This can't be!

My avatar's learning must have evolved

exponentially!'

And apparently

as I dizzily

slapped limply

at my computer keys

researching queasily

his biography

he's as rich as can be!

Living a life of luxury!

He even started his own family!

And named his first child

*after me*!

I dropped my head

in deep dread,

deflated and defeated.

Obviously I taught my avatar

much more than he really needed.

I gazed in a daze

at the image of his face again,

and there it was that silly grin

that I mistook in the past

during my class

thinking his brain was the size of a pin.

But the joke's on me

for now I see

something else in that smile

that one can see

very easily

if you stare at it for a while.

It's not a look of mental deficiency

but one of premeditated chicanery.

For quite obviously,

and very apparently,

he's not grinning vacantly -

he's laughing inside, to himself, at me!

Lightheaded in my hammock,

there's an aching hollowness in my stomach;

my cup's tipped over on the lawn,

my hopes and dreams are shattered and gone.

I think about my classroom time,

and how I had it in my mind

to educate another being,

and what back then I wasn't seeing.

I stare above me

watching the world rock back and forth.

Through the silhouette leaves

I ponder my summer course.

Arrogance, avarice, pride, and greed…

Those are just a few so far…

I swing and think about what I learned,

and the education of my avatar.

# THE HAUNTED TRAMPOLINE

When you live outside of a small town

there aren't many trampolines around.

The one closest to me

belongs to Emily

whose property

has been covered by trees

for at least centuries.

There's a big stone house you can't see

(even though it sits right next to highway three),

a school bus, a deer stand, and an old TV,

a rusty trailer holding a dismantled jet ski,

tires from a tractor, a broken down ATV,

a couch stained with oil and grease,

a tin trough full of brown water and leaves,

a rabbit coop, a bed spring, and a sunken jalopy,

and other stuff hidden by the bushes and weeds.

And that includes

the trampoline.

And it's a very good thing that the trampoline sits properly

at the far corner of Emily's property

as it's been determined by children of both present and past -

you don't want to be closer to the house than that.

It's best to get to the trampoline from the back,

from the forest, where you can find hints of a path.

But it's not like you're exactly safe

because there are poison oak, and poison ivy leading the way,

along with bushes with prickers,

and other plants that can stick ya,

and rusty barbed wire that appears to grow from the ground.

That's why it's always good to look down.

And the path always seems to change,

as if the forest gets rearranged.

But you know you're almost there

when there's an eery chill in the air.

And you break out into an empty clearing

where the land is dry and barren,

where the tramp rests on dead earthen ground,

where the surrounding plants are always brown

as if the trampoline has kept the forest at bay.

No plants grow its way.

Where the trampoline sits

no life exists.

My friends and I always stop before we get too close

for some reason that we don't even know,

like something is making us think about what we're doing,

and if it's not better just to turn around

and keep on moving.

For the tramp looks like a black alien ship

that didn't drop down to say, 'Hi',

but landed as a curse from a dark universe

through a black hole in the sky.

Or it rose out of the ground

in the dead of night when no one was around,

and when night comes again

back it will descend

to where only evil can be found.

These may seem like harsh words

but there are certain things that have occurred.

Like the last time we were here

when Jimmy broke through when the tramp did tear.

We remember that he was high in the air,

and when he landed he wasn't there.

We heard a rip, and a yelp,

and a moaning cry for help.

He broke his leg.

Or the time we were playing Break The Egg,

and Karen was the egg balled up in the middle,

and Darin and Sharon and I were trying to break her cradle.

We bounced her too high,

though we didn't even try,

and she went over the side.

She still has a patch on her eye.

Or when Glen ripped his skin

on a rusty spring,

and Will still has a scar

from when he came down hard

on the metal bar that surrounds the whole thing.

Trampolines these days

have a big net to keep children at bay,

and the places that have metal or springs

are covered by thick padded things.

And there's a safe way to get on 'em,

and a safe way to get off 'em,

and they come with a book filled with lots of precautions.

Emily's tramp has none of those options.

New tramps these days also tend to be small.

Emily's tramp can fit us all.

Like the day long ago

(some kids I didn't even know)

when we didn't know any better

and we all got on the tramp and put our shoes in the middle.

It's a game where you have to leave the tramp

if you get touched by a shoe.

(Three kids ended that day with bruises black and blue.

Someone sprained an ankle, another lost a tooth.)

At the end of the game when we all had our shoes

on the tramp sat a lone pair of boots.

A little girl's cowboy boots from the 1800's

was what scared all of us.

We're not sure how old Emily's tramp is.

Probably built back in the 1970's

or some other time

when they didn't take safety seriously.

Its springs are rusty, the metal bars are too,

and there's always a chance someone might fall through

when the thin fabric rips.

Like it did with Jimmy, or when Jenny fractured her hip.

But Emily's tramp always looks the same,

as if it repairs itself after being jumped on for the day.

Maybe someone from the house

comes out

and fixes it when we're gone.

But we've never seen that done.

(I think the tramp puts itself back together

during nights of lightning and rainy weather.)

When we get to the tramp

there it sits with a slight slant,

its fabric shorn

looking old and worn,

thick metal bars with green chipping paint,

rusty springs that don't sit straight,

waiting for us to get up and ride

as we all gather slowly around its sides.

That's when I feel something on the bar I'm touching.

A name that's scratched into it like a medieval etching.

*Emily,* it reads, which is why we call it her tramp.

Who Emily is (or was) we don't know that.

And who lives in the old house,

we don't know that either.

But it's really not something

we want to discover.

So while we keep a lookout

through the trees toward the house

(no one from the house has ever come out)

someone will climb on and slowly start to bounce.

Someone else will climb on,

and then another, and another, until we've all gone.

We'll get comfortable jumping higher and higher,

playing our games, our talking and laughter getting louder.

And the accidents of the past will slowly be forgotten

as we joyously jump up and down upon it.

They say right before an earthquake

there's a certain type of weather,

it's hot, and still, and the dense air has a tremble.

Yet it's only something recognized

after the earth has quaked and smoke fills the sky.

While we bounce, and laugh, and sing

we don't pay attention to the sound of the springs.

We don't hear the voice that surrounds us:

the squeaky springs echoing through the dense forest stillness

like the crying of spirits rhythmically wailing in chorus.

While we're bouncing and singing our songs

the trampoline, too, is singing along.

# BEING THE LEADER

I don't get many chances

because it just so happens

I'm one of the younger kids.

And it's not because of something I did.

There are just kids that were born before me,

so I let it be, and don't make it a story.

That being so

as you would know

if you were not the oldest,

but not the littlest,

just kind of in the middle of the list,

when it comes to games like Follow The Leader

my position in line is about where you'd figure.

Somewhere near the middle of the line

is where I bide my time

until someone ahead of me loses the queue.

That's when the game is through.

Because if you're the kid following the kid

who's not doing what the Leader just did,

you lost.

That's just the cost

of playing the game.

It isn't a shame.

It's just how it goes

because everyone knows

that the game of Follow The Leader

is best when your leader is keener

on losing everyone.

That's just how the game is done.

That being told

I'm more sold

on being old.

Being old makes you more bold

and more fleet

on your feet.

Overall it's more fun

to have a Leader who can run.

(I've played Follow The Leader

with kids that are littler

and I must say it's kind of boring

because you just end up touring

around the backyard.

And doing that is not very hard.)

With older kids

they make you do things you never before did.

Like climb up fences, and jump over walls,

doing their best to make you fall.

Anyway, the point is,

even though I'm just a middle kid,

I was once picked to lead.

And that made my heart beat

because behind me were going to be older kids

who had to copy everything I did.

So I was determined in my mind

to give everyone the hardest time

and leave everyone behind.

Even the older kids.

So that's what I did.

I took off in a sprint through the nearest hedge,

jumped on a wall and teetered on its edge,

landed on the ground with a roll,

and spun around a telephone pole.

(Hearing the screams and laughter

falling behind me faster and faster!)

Under a car I sprawled,

squeezed through two tight walls,

through a chainlink fence I crawled

(and tore my pants

but never mind that),

swung on a branch

over a can of trash,

leapt over a fire hydrant like a frog,

walked across a wobbly log,

tromped through water in a gutter,

found another car to crawl under,

hopped through a field of rocks,

and then sprinted an entire block.

But when I slowed

to figure out where next to go

I turned to see that I was alone.

No one was behind me

for as far as I could see.

So I waited under a tree

to see if any kids were still following me.

But they weren't

I was certain.

So I sat there waiting

with the heat unabating,

and after awhile,

with my thoughts compiled,

decided to go look for them.

Now that's not how the game should end.

I should be in the center

of everyone declaring me the winner

and giving me the thumbs up finger.

I shouldn't have to walk all the way back to the beginning.

That's just not a part of Follow The Leader winning.

When I got back to where the game started,

everyone had departed.

I was all by myself.

Everyone had gone somewhere else.

No one was there cheering me on,

waiting to tell me that I had won,

and what a great Leader I was,

and how even the older kids I lost,

and that I was the greatest Leader of all time…

When I got to the start, the place was all mine.

Everyone had gone somewhere else to play,

so I spent the day

hunting them down,

kicking stones on the ground,

but none of my friends I found.

So I just walked back to my house

while it was getting dark out.

And I went to bed contemplatively,

wondering if being a leader was all it was cracked up to be.

I wondered if real leaders, like presidents or kings,

ever felt the same thing.

If after a great day of leading was done

were they the only ones

who cared?

And at the ceiling did they stare,

in the bed of their home,

feeling alone?

# A Letter To The Birthday Party Host

Dear moms,

(and dads.

Though I don't see many of those.

Mostly moms are birthday party hosts.

Or moms and their friends.

Or a mom and her sister or some other kin.

But rarely dads.

Which is too bad.

Although, probably, not for the dads.)

I'm writing this letter not to complain,

and I don't want to be a strain

on how birthday parties are run.

I just have a few suggestions,

certain things I want to mention

on how a birthday party should be done.

An alternate way,

let's say,

in which a birthday party can be managed

just so you have an advantage

the next time a birthday comes around

and you can be the favorite of your crowd.

(Or at least a favorite among the kids.

After reading this letter, you'll get my gist.)

It seems these days

there's an odd craze

to have a birthday party where the invitees

are forced, for some reason that I can't clearly see,

to play games.

And not fun games.

Boring games.

Many of those games being homemade.

Like bobbing for apples.

Do I really have to

try and chomp into an apple while it's floating?

I'd rather be boating.

On a yacht.

With people taking pictures of me

with the Great White shark I caught.

Instead of dunking my head into a tub of water.

Why bother?

If I have to go to a party and get wet

then I must confess

a place like Water World would be the best.

And it would be closed

to everyone except the party goers.

With its tubes, and slides, and waves to play in,

and a cafeteria that serves free food where you can dine-in.

So mothers (and fathers)

you see where I'm going with this?

The birthday parties you're providing aren't the best.

Kids these days deserve to have more fun

than playing games invented before World War One.

The other day

I had to play

a game with a pencil and a jar.

I had to drop the pencil from my chin

with the hopes that it would go in -

one of the most boring games by far.

And let's get one thing straight,

this letter isn't sour grapes

because my pencil never went in.

And I'm not embarrassed about the fact

that I placed a donkey's tail

on the birthday girl's back.

Or broke an egg

down my leg.

Or kept falling down in my sack.

I just think you should choose

games that someone like me can't lose.

Like going on a cruise

with everybody getting private rooms.

And we can land in Disneyland.

That would be grand.

You see, it's not rocket science

with the fun you're providing,

you just need to think in a different way,

and give a child, like me, a say.

For instance, here's an idea

with that yacht in the sea.

Along with a pool that's surrounded by sand

it could have a launch pad

with a helicopter that kids can fly,

along with a hovercraft

that goes super fast

while we shoot fireworks into the sky.

What about I trip

on a spaceship?

Like the USS Enterprise?

Picture, if you will,

all the kids thrill

if control of Congress was a prize?

Just for one day?

Imagine all the laws we can change!

You see what I'm getting at?

Instead of being forced to swing a bat

at a decorative sack,

you should think of something more constructive than that.

I mean, it's great that the thing is full of candy

but I think it would be more dandy

if it was full of something useful.

Like gift certificates to get us out of school,

forever.

That would be clever.

And, yes, I'm aware of the fact

that the last time I was blindfolded and handed a bat

and was spun around and twirled

until I nearly hurled

and told to hit a piñata,

it didn't go the way it oughta.

I accidentally let go

and the bat went through the neighbor's window.

(I know.

It was quite a show.

But I've since let it go.)

And certainly cornhole would be better

if the boards were closer together,

and tossing rings

should be done with hula hoop-sized things,

and let's not even mention croquet.

I can think of better ways

to spend the day.

(And not because I always come in last

while everyone watches me play.)

What if, instead, we had a soiree

with a coat-and-tie catered buffet

sailing Old Ironsides around the San Francisco Bay

shooting the cannons at anything that came our way?

Truth be told

we kids are old souls

and have sophisticated needs.

So instead of balloons that fly away in the breeze

and party favors

that have lost their flavor,

and pointy hats

with tight rubber straps,

and other things that don't last

like those blowy things you can blast

that eventually fall apart in your hands,

you can give us things that aren't so outdated.

Imagine the joy it would bring

to give us such things

as Lamborghinis and homes that are gated?

Instead of having a party in your backyard

you could pick us up in a limousine car

and take us to an airport, to a private jet.

That kind of party just hasn't been done yet.

And the jet would take us anywhere we wanted,

like the Bahamas,

or some other place we just picked out of a hat.

How about that?

I don't want to come off as a brat

but there are just some things that your parties are lacking.

Like corporate backing

and other financial sources

that will set you on the right course

so you can afford

games that go beyond just dice and a playing board.

Like an all inclusive stay next to an exotic shore.

Or an around-the-world balloon tour.

Or visiting the Earth's core.

You see, there's so much more

than rolling a ball down a wooden floor.

(I must say bowling would be better

if you got points for getting it in the gutter.)

So, in conclusion, my birthday party host,

let's start having parties where you can boast

that you know how to throw a party!

Today you can get started!

(And just in case I made a fuss

I'm signing this)

*Anonymous*

(What about a private bus?

For all of us?

That can turn into a submarine?

And it has an IMAX movie screen,

and paintball, and pinball machines,

and we can float through an ocean never before seen

that still has marine life in it from the Triassic and Pleistocene?

And let's not forget

the all-you-can-eat pizza, soda dispenser, and self-serve ice cream!)

P.S. That would be keen.

# My Best Friend

Bigfoot is my best friend

and no one even knows that.

No one even knows that

because they'd never understand

that my best friend in the whole wide world

is one part ape and one part man.

He's nine feet tall because I measured him once,

and weighs a thousand pounds, probably to the ounce.

When I sit on my side of the teeter-totter

with every rock I've found,

his side of the teeter-totter never leaves the ground.

We jump, and we hop, and we pick wildflowers.

Walk over logs and play in waterfall showers.

We roll down hills, and giggle, and laugh,

and chase each other through forest paths.

We play hide-and-seek, and tic-tac-toe,

hit each other with snowballs when there's snow.

Ahead of me he walks and I try to follow in his steps.

(To be quite honest, I haven't been able to do it yet.)

Over fields of boulders

he carries me on his shoulders.

I look at the ground

that's a long way down

and say, 'Don't drop me!'

as he hops from rock to rock so fleetingly.

'Like a mountain goat!' I tell him, bouncing on his back.

He stops, and looks up at me, and grunts,

'What's that?'

I say, 'Never mind,'

and kick his sides.

'Keep going!'

And he laughs fully knowing

that he's scaring me to death

as he jumps faster and faster

while I scream and hold my breath.

In the soft meadow grass

we sit back to back

(I feel like I'm sitting against a big fur mat!)

taking a break from our day of fun.

In one big bite he eats the sandwich I brought him.

While he's asking me if I have another

I stand up (but he's still taller)

and jump on his back

in sudden attack!

(But he's so huge

he doesn't even move!)

He picks me up and spins around

like a helicopter over the ground.

He puts me in a tree way up high,

grunts, 'Jump!', and off I fly!

Even though it gives me a scare

as I fall faster through the air,

his big arms, thick with hair,

will always be there

to catch me with care;

with my head still spinning from the speed

he gently places me on my feet.

He likes to play Leap Frog but it's kind of lopsided

as over me he easily glides

with his legs spread but not very wide,

and he'll touch my shoulders just to be nice

and hop a bit

(though he doesn't need to do any of it).

I, on the other hand,

have to jump on him, and with both hands

grab his fur, and climb up his back,

to reach his neck and shoulders, pulling on anything I can,

just to get to his head and drop off the other side.

(Even though he's squatting like a frog

it's still really high.)

Sometimes we'll sit with our bare feet together.

(His feet feel like old thick leather.)

I'll line up my feet

wondering how many of my feet equals one of his.

Which is about four and a little bit.

He'll grunt, 'Hold on to my toes!'

and suddenly we're doing a double forward roll,

and over and over we go!

However, here lies the real problem

with being Bigfoot's buddy,

besides coming home tired,

dirty, wet, and muddy.

People think he doesn't exist,

and those that do aren't totally convinced.

I used to argue, I used to cry,

I used to pout,

and roll about,

stomping, and shouting, 'He's alive, HE'S ALIVE!'

We used to laugh at this, how I used to be,

tossing stones into a river, Bigfoot sitting next to me.

'Remember,' he'd grunt, 'when you tried to convince

all the people that I did exist?'

'Yes,' I'd say, kind of shy.

He'd put his big arm around me and wink an eye.

'It's alright, little friend, just so you know,

you don't have to convince others to like your show.'

He'd hiccup and burp a bit.

(By that time I was used to it.)

'You're who you are and that's all that matters.

You don't have to listen to all the chatter.'

Well the years have passed, and time has moved on,

my playdates with Bigfoot are now long gone.

But I know he's out there, I can hear him growling

when there's thunder, and lightning, and the wind is howling.

I know he's out there when darkness is falling,

I know he's out there, I can hear him calling.

I know he's out there when the sun is shining,

when the birds are chirping, I hear him chiming,

'My pal, my buddy, my best friend

my memories of you will never end!'

Every so often I'll call back

when I'm alone in the forest on some faraway track.

I'll call with a bark, a hoot, and a holler

the language he taught me when I was a toddler.

'I love you Bigfoot! I'll never forget

all the fun times together we spent!'

I'll wait for an answer

but I know his response,

he'll leave me in silence in my unwavering stance.

He'll make me listen to nothing,

nothing at all…

He'll make me doubt, he'll make me wonder -

did I imagine everything we did together?

I'll listen harder in his wilderness

only to hear his quiet stillness.

I'll give up and get really sad

that maybe I imagined those times we had.

I'll take a step, and then I'll stop,

certain I heard something beyond my thoughts.

Another step I'll take, and then another,

thinking for sure that I heard a murmur.

I'll take another step, a step, and a step,

I'll feel the birds singing, and hear the sun set.

I'll smell the fall of water across the rocks,

taste the scent of flowers,

the chamomile, the hollyhocks.

I'll see the trees looking down

at all the animals prancing around.

I'll start to skip, and then I'll run,

remembering my pal and all of our fun!

I'll pretend I'm chasing Bigfoot, or he's chasing me,

running through the forest like it used to be!

I'll push my feet upon the ground

and feel the Earth spin around!

Suddenly I'll break out in an uncontrollable grin

because I know how this world spins!

Harder I'll run, and harder I'll push,

making the world pass with a glorious *Whoosh!*

Faster, and faster, until I'm laughing in fits,

because I know, I know, I know for sure:

*I'm the one who's spinning it!*

# Sisters of Gold

It just so happened, by some twist of fate,

I was alone in the house, and it was late.

My parents had just left on vacation

which left my sisters the vocation

of taking care of me.

Which is fine as can be

because they really never have anything planned.

As far as rules go, I'm a free man.

I can do whatever I want,

like play video games from dusk 'til dawn

which, one night, I tried to do.

Well, I didn't even make it until two.

I think I even fell asleep before ten.

(Probably from all the ice cream I had eaten before then.)

As far as babysitters go, my sisters are great.

They don't care if I stay up late.

In fact, when it comes to me, they don't care at all,

they care more about their latest tweet, text, or smart phone call.

And between the two of them they don't really talk,

which was why when one of them went for a walk

to go to a friend's house at the end of the block,

the other had no idea she was gone.

(You can probably guess where this night's going.)

So when the sister that was left with me all alone

shouted at the closed door of an empty room,

'I'm spending the night at Kellie's, so you have to babysit!'

she never realized her sister had already split.

Oblivious to it all

I never heard any of their calls

because I was deep in a video,

with my headphones on, listening to my race car go.

From my game, I went straight to bed

with the notion still in my head

that both of my sisters were in the house.

One in her room, the other on the couch.

When I woke up in the middle of the night

I still didn't know of my sisters' flight,

and that I was in my home

all alone -

eight years old, by myself,

with no one's help.

What woke me up were voices that weren't very far,

somewhere deep in my backyard.

So I snuck out of bed, and crawled to my window,

and saw some movement under the full moon's glow.

Four men were in the light of a lantern,

and one them looked like a pirate ship captain.

He had a wooden peg leg, and one hand was a hook,

in his other hand a sword he shook

at the ground,

grumbling, 'Put it down,

we'll bury it here!'

It was summer, and my window was open,

that's why I could hear.

My backyard backs up to a swampy delta

that leads out into the ocean,

which is why I want to tell ya

I was startled to see the commotion.

Nothing ever happens out there

because it's a place where you have to beware

of all the snakes, and all the gators.

People have gone out there and never come back

wearing their fishing waders.

My backyard doesn't have a fence,

only foliage that's very dense,

and I don't think those men out there

realized that my house was so near.

'Aye, aye, Captain,' I heard one of them say.

'We'll get it buried before the day.'

'Sooner than that!' the captain growled.

'How do you know we weren't being followed?'

*'Braawk! How do you know we weren't being followed?'*

the parrot on his shoulder squawked and hollered.

'Shut yer mouth bird!'

was what I heard,

and from the bird

not another word

because shining at the end of its beak

was the captain's hook that ended its speech.

So it went for at least an hour

as behind my window I did cower,

watching the four men bury something out there,

and wondered if my sisters were aware.

(Because, of course, I still didn't know at the time

that both of my sisters were gone for the night.)

It was after midnight

when, with their lantern light,

they got back in their black dory boat.

As they drifted into the night

I saw painted on the boat's side

a skull and white skeleton bones.

Of course I couldn't sleep,

so out of my room I did creep,

and snuck out there with a flashlight and shovel,

and found the place where it looked like something was covered.

The sky was starting to glow

while I snuck around because I still didn't know

that my sisters were gone.

And it took me until dawn

to drag in the heavy chest

that I took to deposit

in the back of my closet,

then I went to bed to rest.

I didn't wake up until late

because there were no sounds to make me awake.

Like my sisters playing loud music in their rooms,

which is why I didn't wake up until noon,

wondering if what happened until morning's light

was something I might have dreamt during the night.

But the tracks on the floor

that led to my closet door

had me remembering more,

like what was buried by the four.

When I opened my closet

I nearly lost it!

There it was, shoved in the corner,

with its old wood panels and naval brass borders.

Oh, yes!

A treasure chest!

I crawled to it slowly on my hands and knees

through toys, and shoes, and clothes hanging over me.

The lid was so heavy that I needed both hands

to lift it up and get a glance

of just exactly what was inside of it.

That's when my face and eyes alit!

I shut the lid fast

and then fell back

not believing it was true!

I had a real treasure chest full of treasure

hidden in my room!

I slowly opened the lid again,

and a shimmering light the contents sent,

filling my closet with a golden light

from all the treasure shining bright!

Coins, and emeralds, diamonds, and bracelets,

crowns, and rubies, and gold bar ingots!

Cannikins, chains, plates, and spoons,

thimbles, and trinkets, and Spanish doubloons!

Goblets, amulets, beads, and rings,

pearl necklaces, buttons, and gold figurines!

Everything a treasure chest could possibly hold

filled to the brim with jewelry and gold!

With a shaky hand I pulled out a piece

that looked like it came from an ancient place.

A gold brooch of a sword-wielding ruby-eyed dragon.

I wondered with a chill what kind of person it would hang on.

A king, or a warrior,

a czar, or an emperor?

Maybe a pharaoh had it first

and centuries later an evil queen gave it a curse.

I put it back, and shut the lid,

and away from the chest I slowly slid

thinking I might be the luckiest kid

to have ever lived!

The next few hours required some stealth.

(Still not realizing I was by myself.)

I had to erase my path, and cover my tracks,

through the yard, and through the house,

from the treasure I had dragged.

Out by the water, the hole I covered,

filling it with dirt, and hiding it in foliage.

I cleaned everything up to my closet door.

I even mopped the kitchen floor.

(Something I had never done before.

And would never do again, I swore.)

I was sitting at the table having a fine meal

of my favorite cereal

when a sister walked in,

the youngest named Kim.

She was making her breakfast

of eggs, bacon, and ketchup

when we heard the front door shut.

Kim and I both looked up.

Who could that be?

Did Mom and Dad come home early?

It was Ginger,

my other sister,

who came in

and threw her purse next to Kim's.

It didn't occur to me,

because I had turned on the TV,

that Ginger and Kim

were wearing the same things

they were wearing the day before.

Their communication I did ignore

as they looked at each other nervously

and then talked to each other angrily

in low voices so I couldn't hear.

But from what I gathered passively

their conversation was quite clear.

It was about me being left by myself

and my parents they wouldn't tell.

But I was in my own special world

while around me their talk and the television swirled.

I had a chest full of treasure in my room!

And I was thinking of all the things I could do!

Out of the kitchen I flew!

I didn't even finish my food!

(Hearing behind me my sisters calling each other names

and who it should be to take the blame.)

I caused a bit of scuttlebutt

because I spent the day in my room with the door shut.

My sisters were now worried about me,

due to, I believed, both of them feeling guilty.

They wouldn't stop knocking and asking me politely

if there was anything I needed and they'd go fetch it kindly.

Which I took full advantage of, have no doubt.

'I need another snack!' I often did shout.

I think by the end of the day they were both worn out,

but decided that I had never known about,

and therefore would never tell my parents about,

the fact that they had left me alone,

all by myself, for an entire night, in an empty home.

But in my mind, for them, the day was fine practice

because their lives they were going to have to readjust.

They now lived with a king

who had a treasure of his own,

and they were going to be my servants

while I sat upon my throne.

The next day everything was back to normal

with my sisters doing all the things they did before.

Like hang out in front of the television, or in their rooms,

ignoring me, and letting me do whatever I wanted to do.

Which was be a king.

Because here's the thing.

The day before

I took to explore

all the treasure in the chest

to figure out what a king would wear

and what on me would look the best.

I found a crown that fit me perfectly

as if it were made just for me.

(The bejeweled crown of gold

was probably really old,

because when it was made

people were smaller in those days.)

I found necklaces, bracelets, and rings that also fit.

(Probably owned by a princess or two,

but that didn't bother me a bit.)

By the end of my dress-up

I had the perfect get-up

and was the finest king in the land.

There was no doubt

people would bow

when I flourished my royal hand.

Walking down the hall

I felt real tall

as if I had grown much bigger.

My status as king

had become the real thing

just as I had figured.

I was hoping for more of a reception

as I entered the kitchen,

like my sisters prepping my buffet of food.

But they weren't there,

and I wondered if they were aware

that treating their king like that was rude.

My servants were nowhere to be found

which was no way to obey the crown.

So I sat down at the head of the table

and yelled, 'I would like a PB&J, and some chips,

and a pie made out of apple!'

I clapped twice and shouted, *'Hello?'*,

but still there was no answer.

'You're king is hungry and needs some food!

Come and feed your master!'

That's when Kim walked in

with a look that was grim

and asked, 'Who are you shouting at?

And where did you get that hat?

And what the heck?

Is that Mom's fur shawl around your neck?

And why are you wearing Dad's robe?

That's what I want to know.

And where did you get all that jewelry? Is that Mom's too?

What's gotten into you?'

'It's my jewelry,' I said.

'And bow your head

when you approach your king.

You should be on one knee

before talking to me

and kissing my royal ring.'

I presented a hand with covered fingers,

and I must say, then, that Kim's interest lingered.

Each finger had a ring or two,

and on my wrist, many bracelets too.

'You better put Mom's jewelry back before she returns.

And if you get Dad's robe dirty you're going to learn

not to mess with our parents stuff when they're away

or you'll be grounded for forever and a day.

And are those Mom's nice leather boots?

You better take those off right now too!'

(I must confess Mom's boots

gave my height a little boost.)

'I told you, Kim, this is all mine.

Not the clothes, of course, but everything that shines.

You think mom would have jewelry like this?'

I said pointing to the ruby-eyed dragon brooch

bordered by the gold snakes that twist.

'Our parents can't afford the treasure I wear

because I'm a king, not a peasant, as you should be aware.'

With my brooch Kim's attention was caught,

and closer to me she got.

'Where'd you get that?'

she asked.

But the moment was broken when Ginger walked in

saying with a mocking grin,

'Who's this sitting at the table?

It looks like someone took a king

and shrunk him down to a little thing,

like something out of a fable.'

At least she said *king*

was what I was thinking.

'That's right, I'm a king.

*Your* king to be exact.

Now you two need to learn how to obey me,

and how, in front of your king, you should act.

First things first, I need some lunch,

like a tuna melt sandwich with fries to munch.

Or maybe you two should fire up the grill

and cook me a burger with a soda to swill.

Pancakes are fine any time of the day.

Or mac and cheese with grape Kool-Aid—'

Ginger interrupted and said,

while taking the crown from my head,

'Where did you get this thing?

From Burger King?

Since when did they make them so heavy?'

Kim said, 'Maybe the thick-headed kids

get thicker ones.

That's why his is so heavy.'

Ginger said, 'Our parents are coming back in two days

so you better put all their clothes away

before you get them soiled with food and Kool-Aid.

Which we're not making for you, by the way.

And put Mom's jewelry back before you lose it.

If anything's missing she'll have a true fit.

And let's be clear

you need to stop shouting in our ears.

You're not a king, you're just a little kid.

So about this king stuff, shut your lid.'

A typical speech Ginger would give.

(She thinks she's the boss because she's the oldest kid.)

They both left, the last being Kim,

nodding her head at me with an agreeing grin.

'This jewelry is mine and I'm your king!' I shouted,

but they didn't listen,

because, by then, they were both out of the kitchen.

Leaving me solo to get my own food

which wasn't easy in high-heeled boots.

My bracelets were so heavy I could barely lift my hands.

With all my jewelry I must have gained twenty pounds.

Which is why a king shouldn't have to do a thing

but sit on his throne and tap his fingers covered with rings.

I found a perfect home

for my royal throne.

The attic in our garage

was my choice for a king to lodge.

It contains Grandma's old chair that's high-backed with armrests,

and there's a window

where I can look down upon the rest.

How I'd get my treasure up there was another matter,

the garage only had a pull-down ladder.

I was on my last legs

with all the trips I had to take.

But by the end of the day all was set,

so I sat on my throne and had a much deserved rest.

I looked out the window at my sprawling domain

thinking that soon that swampy delta will be called by my name.

And perhaps even more.

Like everything from shore to shore

that in due time

will be all mine,

for I'm the richest king in the world!

I must have fallen asleep,

and it must have been deep,

because the light was gone

when I woke up on my throne.

My royal room was dark, and so was the outside,

so it must have been sometime into the night

when I heard a scream, and it wasn't from delight.

Out my stately window

I saw a lantern light glow.

That's when I got a sickness in my stomach

because in pirates' arms my sisters were clutched!

With their tricorn hats,

and silk belt sashes,

they waved their swords

to the captain's words,

'Take these wenches back to the ship

for they're the one's who took our treasure!

We'll throw them into the bilge

and lock them up for bad behavior!'

I watched, frozen,

with my mouth wide open

as my sisters were put into a boat,

and away the pirates rowed!

I must say

that being a king has its bad days.

Like the next day I spent

cleaning out our old rowboat with dents,

and trying to figuring out

how I was going to go about

getting my sisters before my parents returned,

and before they learned

that their daughters had been taken by pirates.

(I'm sure they wouldn't admire it.)

Have you ever tried to bargain with a pirate?

Especially when that pirate is irate?

With an eye patch, and a furious gaze,

while in front of you a sharp hook he shakes,

wondering who'd be brave enough to take

the bounty of a pirate?

How would you go about it?

Well, here's what I did,

and it took a lot of thought,

because, occasionally, kings have to do things

that can't be taught.

It was well into the evening,

with my rowing and heavy breathing,

when I came upon their ship,

and by sharp sword tips

was escorted to the captain

while carrying the suitcases I had put the treasure in.

You see, I put the treasure in

the suitcases of Ginger and Kim

so the pirate captain would think

that the treasure didn't belong to him,

and that his treasure was somewhere still out there yet,

in his own treasure chest.

And just to prove that the treasure I had

wasn't the treasure he once had,

I put in a watch given to me by my grandad.

Even though it looked like gold, it wasn't real gold,

but I didn't think that would be something a pirate would know.

The captain also wouldn't know

that the watch stopped working long ago,

because I don't think pirates even know what a watch is.

Thank goodness.

So sweating, and fearful,

and after a dreadful earful

of how he was going to make me walk the plank,

and turn my sisters into slaves, and not give them back,

I opened the suitcase with the watch on top.

That's when he stopped.

I hung the watch on his hook.

'See, Captain, look.

Now do you understand?

This is a different treasure than the treasure you once had.

And if you didn't know, I'm the king of this land.

And I need my servants back.

Because they're mine.

And *your* treasure is somewhere else out there to find.

So in my servants places

you can have these suitcases

which means that if you ever find your other stash

you're going to have double the treasure in your stack.'

His parrot squawked back,

*'Double the treasure!'*

The captain's eyes lit up in pleasure.

At the dinner table I'm now stationed.

My parents are back from their vacation

asking my sisters how the babysitting went,

and how their time was spent,

and if there was any dissent, or discontent.

That's when my sisters looked sternly at me,

and then at each other, and I could plainly see

that the looks they were giving each other

silently said they couldn't tell on their brother.

They couldn't tell my parents

that they were almost pirate slaves,

and that their suitcases had gone away,

because they left me alone for an entire night

and half of a day.

And I'm only eight.

That's when I decided to clear the air

and relieve my parents of their cares.

My sisters were giving me sour stares

when I said, 'Mom,' then said, 'Dad,

Ginger and Kim are the best babysitters I've ever had.

Nothing happened.

All was grand.'

While under the table I held

the ruby-eyed dragon in my hand.

# P-I-G

I think if I was called a pig

and I really was a pig

my feelings wouldn't be hurt, I think.

Because I don't think pigs know they're pigs,

they're just pigs, I think.

And not to make a stink,

but if I were a pig, I'd think, *This is great!*

Nothing would make me irate!

I would just be one, big, happy pig!

Being a pig would be my only gig!

You'd never see me frown

as I chowed down,

smiling the whole day long,

putting the pounds on!

Eating everything that came my way,

and everyday would be the same!

I'd never complain!

I'd wake up each day and claim,

'What am I going to eat today?'

as I waddled out to play

in the fields

looking for my next meal!

Spinach, and carrots,

yams, and asparagus,

squash, and pumpkin!

Anything I could munch on!

With my big pig nose

I'd snort around for anything that grows!

I'd eat straight from the earth

to build my girth,

even if it was covered in dirt!

Like truffles!

Into my mouth those I'd shovel!

They wouldn't call me a pig for nothin'

while I ate all the buttons

of garlic,

and when I was done

my lips I'd lick!

Along with turnips, and beets,

potatoes that are sweet!

Plowing through every crop,

I wouldn't stop!

Eating!

All day long I'd be feeding!

To my trough I'd trot

wondering what I got!

Wheat, or oats,

old baked beans, or toast,

cabbage from a roast

soaking in the sourest of creams!

What a dream!

Filled up by the farmer

or his daughter,

it wouldn't matter

who filled my platter!

Banana peels?

Bread heels?

It's time to squeal,

'It's all a meal!'

A bucket or two

of rotten food

would make my curly tail wiggle

while I giggled

and grunted!

I wouldn't even care if I was the runt of

the litter!

What's for dinner?

Or breakfast? Or lunch?

How about brunch?

And what's that meal called between lunch and dinner?

*Linner?*

Whatever it's called

I'd finish her!

No doubt

I'd just pig out

and feast the hours away

into one glorious, gluttonous day!

Corn husks, corn hulls,

rotted corn on the stalk,

I'd eat it all, I wouldn't balk!

I'd fill myself from head to toe,

hock to hock,

all the slop!

I'd never stop!

Watermelon, lemon, orange, and cheese rinds!

How many rinds could I find?

All of them if I had the time!

Onion, cucumber, potato skins,

give me everything in the compost bin!

I'd win awards

for being the biggest pig in the whole wide world!

Wearing my blue ribbons

I'd eat everything I'm given!

I'd put my eating to the test

doing my best to out-eat the rest

at the State Fair

where I'd eat more than my fair share

because it's all delicious fare!

Buffalo wings, French fries, fried mac and cheese,

ice cream sandwiches I'd eat with ease!

Beer battered cheese curds, donuts,

fried pickles, honey roasted nuts,

shaved ice, waffle sticks,

funnel cake, briskets,

cotton candy, corndogs!

I'd be the biggest hog!

While my owner held his trophy

into the truck they'd shove me

with the kids shouting, '*Yuk!*',

as I rolled around in my muck!

Back at the farm

I'd eat everything within the reach of my arm,

following my nose

wherever it goes,

eating anything that grows!

Or didn't grow, or couldn't grow

because it's weeks old!

I'd be a gourmand

eating whatever my owners didn't want!

You want to get rid of it?

I'll find a place for it to fit!

You say that cottage cheese is weeks old?

I'm sold!

I'll take the rest

of that soggy lettuce!

You think those eggs are rotten?

I'll take them all if you got 'em!

Do you have any more of that leftover cake

by mistake?

Even if the frosting's hard and the inside's moldy,

that's a chance I'm willing to take!

I'll eat it boldly!

Those sausages that are just the ends

with bites taken out of them?

I'll eat all of 'em!

And to drink?

Anything you can think!

Fermented orange juice with curdled milk,

I'd slurp it all up until I got my fill!

And then I'd drink more

to uneven the score!

I'd even drink water

as long as it had food scraps floating on it!

And just when I thought I could eat another bite

I'd call it a night!

With the sun setting low

down I'd go

into a nice bath of mud

thinking about my day of grub!

I'd hit the hay

and snore away

in my big pig way,

dreaming about the next day's buffet!

And what would you call me?

I'd have no idea!

Even if you called me by it!

I'd be too busy working on my diet!

You can even spell it out

if there was any doubt,

but I'd be too concerned about stuffing my mouth

to care about

my name

while my weight gained!

I would live so heavenly

in a world that is my eatery

as one big happy

*p-i-g*!

# The Curious Case Of The Snowflake

In case you haven't heard

there's been a curious word

about snowflakes

and the form they take.

Even by those smart in the head

it's been said

that *no two snowflakes look the same.*

Isn't that insane?

How is it possible to make that call?

Did someone look at them all?

That I doubt.

Did someone go on a very long walk during a snowfall

as a scout?

With a microscope in hand?

I don't think that's ever been planned.

Even if someone had the time to take

to look at all the snowflakes,

in a storm let's say,

how many snowflakes could a person look at in a day?

Certainly not every one.

I don't think that's ever been done.

Have you ever held a handful of snow packed together?

It's impossible to separate one snowflake from the other.

Even if there was a way to separate a handful of flakes,

how long would that take?

Probably a long time.

At least into the night.

And when you were done

you'd be frozen.

Because it's not like you can study snowflakes

in a place that's warm.

You'd have to do it in a storm.

Or in a room that's really cold.

At least 32 degrees or below.

So who is the fellow

who likes to bellow

that *no two snowflakes look the same?*

That's a bold claim.

When I'm told

that *no two snowflakes look alike*

I want to tell that person to go take a hike.

Like, to the North Pole

where it's really cold

and there's snow everywhere.

I'd tell that person to start there.

And to make sure that with my argument I followed through,

I'd be there too,

to tell that person, 'Listen,

I realize you've made a certain decision

to say that *no two snowflakes look alike*,

but I just don't see how you can be right.

Look around you, there are snowflakes for miles!'

But I'd say this with a smile

because I wouldn't want to hurt that person's feelings.

I'd just want to show them with whom they're dealing.

I'd pick up some snow and say,

'Person,

I'm not trying to be coercive,

just realistic.

How many snowflakes are in my hand do you think?'

(Of course, while asking this,

what couldn't be dismissed

would be the obvious fact that snowflakes are falling all around us!)

'Person,' I'd say, 'I don't think this needs to be discussed!'

But this is just a scenario

as far as discussions go,

and just a suggestion

that when someone mentions

that *no two snowflakes look alike*

you might want to ask them, 'Where's the science?'

If the statement's going to be made

that *no two snowflakes are the same*

looking at everyone of them

would be scientifically pertinent.

Because, as you would know if you were a scientist,

and not just a snowflake theorist,

science takes proof if

you're going to make something conclusive.

So if you're a scientist who wants to prove it

you better start moving it!

Because, right now, I'm sure, somewhere on this globe

there's falling snow!

If science is real

and you're going to make the appeal

that *no two snowflakes look the same*

you better have a jet plane

that can fly from pole to pole in one day.

And to Siberia, and Outer Mongolia,

and to Alaska, and Canada,

and probably Patagonia.

And to all the mountain tops

where the snow never stops.

And how are you going to do that?

You'd have to split yourself in half.

Or into one hundred fifths

to take all those trips.

And what about looking at all the snowflakes from the past?

How are you going to do that?

If you ask me

looking at all the snowflakes in history

is an impossibility!

But just to be compliant

to science

and to prove my stance,

one day I watched a snowflake land in my hand.

I held it up to my nose

and looked at it up close.

The snowflake had six sides that looked like spikes,

and on those spikes were other spikes

that looked like tiny triangles of ice.

I kept that snowflake in my mind

as I held out my mitten for another to find.

A perfect snowflake landed

and that one, too, I examined.

'See!' I said to myself, 'This one has six sides too!'

But I wasn't through.

For to be a scientist I had to be thorough.

So I looked closely at the six sides

and they, too, had triangle spikes.

I must say that the spikes were different.

The triangles were in another arrangement.

But so what?

It didn't mean I was going to give up!

So I did it again, and again.

And you know what?

When I was done

I looked at twenty-three snowflakes because I counted them.

And just because all the snowflakes that I looked at

didn't look the same

doesn't mean that their twin didn't fall somewhere else that day.

So the next day I counted even more.

I looked at so many snowflakes I got bored.

And just because the snowflakes I looked at didn't look alike,

with their six sides and icy triangle spikes

(I even saw long ones

that looked like columns.

But they all looked different too)

and I really couldn't disprove

that *no two snowflakes look the same* out there,

and that my experiment failed

because I couldn't find a pair,

and that perhaps there are certain discontinuities

in atmospheric fluidities

and environmental incongruities

that create complexities for each snowflake that falls

affecting its growth and all,

I would just say

that at the end of the day

(and just to be fair

to all the snowflake pairs

that might be out there)

to say that *no two snowflakes look the same…*

I'm going to leave that saying

up in the air.

# A Thought

Maybe you're reading this in a chair,

or lying in your bed,

hiding under the covers with a phone next to your head.

Maybe you're on a couch,

or at the kitchen table,

or sprawled out on the floor

with headphones and a cable.

Maybe you're looking at a television,

or at a computer screen,

or rocking in a hammock

about to drift off in a dream.

Maybe you copied these words

and wrote them down on paper,

or put them in a notebook so you could read them later.

Are you reading from a book?

From a photograph you took?

In a plane?

On a train?

Under an umbrella to keep off the rain?

Let's just take a moment

to think of these things just mentioned.

Chairs, and beds, and kitchens, and tables,

words, and airplanes, headphones, and cables;

televisions, trains, couches, and cameras,

computers, books, umbrellas, and hammocks.

Have you ever thought about where things come from?

How they came to be?

Perhaps we can answer this question

with a little philosophy.

Didn't all these things start off as a thought?

Of course they did, how could they not?

Someone had to think of a chair

before they began to build it.

A train just doesn't grow out of the ground

like barley, wheat, and millet.

Can airplanes pop out of thin air?

Do kitchens just appear there?

The pieces and parts to make a computer

must have required a thought or two,

someone didn't just open up a drawer and out a computer flew.

Unless televisions and phones grow on trees,

someone had to think about how to make these.

Headphones, umbrellas, tables, and couches

weren't created by mental slouches.

All these things took preconceived thinking.

(And probably some doodling, dabbling, and tinkering!)

That being said -

don't all things begin in the head?

For something to come into being

it must mean

it first starts off

as a thought.

And if that's true

then we must conclude

that thoughts can create!

Isn't that great?

And amazing!

That with a thought we can create a thing!

What about concepts, constructs, methods, and hypotheses,

things that are created that you can't really see?

Rudiments of a government,

how we tell the time,

the rules of a game,

didn't they come from a mind?

The birds, the flowers, and the trees?

Did someone or something think of these?

And how does a thought form?

That's a brainstorm.

How do we think of something never before thought of?

What exactly is the creative process?

How thoughts come to be

is an amusing mystery

whose discovery

might never be,

for the intricacies

of the brain's processes

can go on for eternity!

Like everything above us in the night sky,

there will always be more than meets the eye!

But thoughts are wonderful things.

They can even think up things to sing.

Like in a musical show

with a piano.

(And who thought of that?

Whoever thought of the piano

must be one cool cat!)

So if thoughts create things isn't that something?

That with just your thoughts you can create something?

Which means from nothing for a thing to be something

somewhere, somehow, someone had to think something.

And doesn't that mean that you can create something out of nothing?

So what are you thinking,

what will you make,

in that mind of yours that's yours to create?

Maybe you'll think of something tasty to bake,

or a way to clean up a polluted lake,

or how to drive a car to the stars!

You can't take your thinking too far!

For if thoughts create things

and things come from thoughts

just think…

of how powerful you are.